D1076175

THROWAWAYS

When eleven-year-old Sky and her younger brother Chip are abandoned by their penniless parents they have no idea what will happen to them.

They must find food and somewhere to live, and in an uncharitable world they are pleased to find someone to help them. Dig, who befriends Sky and Chip, takes them to the rubbish dump where abandoned children live in a huge shanty town. There they must live the lives of 'throw-aways', but Sky is determined to find a way to escape this appalling existence . . .

ABOUT THE AUTHOR

Ian Strachan is not only a writer, but also a radio journalist. He had his own chat show on a local radio station in Stoke for twelve years and is currently a producer for BBC Manchester. He has been writing books since 1981.

Ian Strachan's novels show a depth of compassion for the less fortunate and he is not afraid to tackle world-wide problems in his writing. However, he has travelled very little – his first trip abroad was when he went to China and Hong Kong to research one of his books.

Ian Strachan lives with his wife and two children in Staffordshire.

Other titles by Ian Strachan in New Windmills:

The Flawed Glass

Throwaways

IAN STRACHAN

HEINEMANN
NEW WINDMILLS

Heinemann Educational
a division of
Heinemann Publishers (Oxford) Ltd
Halley Court, Jordan Hill, Oxford OX2 8EJ
OXFORD LONDON EDINBURGH
MADRID ATHENS BOLOGNA PARIS
MELBOURNE SYDNEY AUCKLAND SINGAPORE TOKYO
IBADAN NAIROBI HARARE GABARONE
PORTSMOUTH NH (USA)

First published in Great Britain by Methuen Children's Books 1992

First published in the New Windmill Series 1994

94 95 96 97 98 10 9 8 7 6 5 4 3 2 1

ISBN 0 435 12413 7

British Library Cataloguing in Publication Data
for this title is available from the British Library

Cover illustration by Bruce Hogarth

Typeset by CentraCet Limited, Cambridge
Printed and bound in England by Clays Ltd, St Ives plc

The poor don't count, so don't count the poor.

A comment on the exclusion of 5 million Americans from the 1990 census.

The sort of people you step over when you come out of the opera.

A comment on London beggars, 1991.

Naturally, nobody really knows how many street children there are, but UNICEF believe a minimum of one hundred thousand million earn some sort of living on the streets of the world and at least half of those will have no form of shelter to sleep under. But, they add, these figures may be greatly underestimated.

This book is dedicated to them.

One

On the day her life changed for ever, Sky woke early.

Swimming up from the bottom of her private sea, she came to slowly, rubbing her eyes, extracting her legs from under her little brother's. Sky stretched as much as she was able along the back seat of their car which was gritty with dried crumbs and sticky from patches of spilt Cola.

The first rays of daylight were making the mist on the car windows, from the breath of the four sleeping people, blush to the pinky-gold of the inside of a conch shell.

Sky, her little brother Chip, and her parents, had been sleeping in the car for months while they wandered back and forth across the country chasing rumours of work.

They had found some jobs, chopping wood or picking fruit, but nothing which lasted, or which paid enough to feed them all properly, let alone afford somewhere to sleep.

They'd never intended to become vagrants.

When Sky's dad lost the job he'd worked at solidly for ten years he'd started phoning round straight away. Eventually, on the promise of a new job, they'd handed the house keys back to the landlord and set out in their beaten-up, old, brown car on a four hundred mile journey. But, when they arrived, the firm had gone broke and Dad hadn't enough petrol money to get them back home. So, they just kept moving on, listening in cafés and bars and asking at petrol stations for any news of work.

A couple of times Mum and Dad had got work together. Once it was evenings in a sort of café-bar. Dad washed up dishes and pans while Mum waited on table, but they got thrown out when Dad objected to the customers making passes at his wife; thrown out without wages after they'd been working there nearly four days.

But Sky was relieved when that particular job ended. She'd hated trying to sleep in the car parked behind the café while her parents were inside working. Threatening shadows of drunks had drifted across the windows and the car dipped and swayed when they used it as a bench. She used to lie there in the dark, listening to the singing and fighting, terrified to move in case they heard her and tried to break in.

It was soon after that job folded that Dad started getting drunk and Mum went very quiet.

On top of everything else, their car broke down.

It had been coughing and snorting for weeks. The radiator was leaking and they kept stopping in clouds of steam and having to beg water, or scoop it out of ponds.

But then it got really serious.

They were driving along, miles from anywhere. Ahead of them, on the distant horizon, the outline of the city they were trying to reach, quivered in the heat haze.

Suddenly, there was a shattering explosion from the engine and the car, filled with the horrible smell of hot metal and burnt oil, juddered to a halt beside the road.

Dad cursed under his breath as he climbed out to look under the bonnet. When he came back he just slumped down in his seat and sat there leaving the door wide open. "Piston's gone," he said, gazing at the far-off city outline. "Blown a hole right through the side of the engine."

Sky remembered that was the first time she'd heard Mum sound frightened. "What do we do now?" she'd asked.

"Well, we're not going anywhere any more, not in this!" The lines on Dad's face looked deeper.

"To look at me," he used to say, "you'd never think I was thirty-eight!" and Mum would laugh. That day he looked more like sixty and Sky couldn't remember when she'd last heard Mum laugh.

It was hot and still. No traffic passed. Two big, black flies buzzed noisily as they chased each other up the windscreen.

Slowly Mum climbed out of the car and walked round to lean against the open bonnet, without bothering to look at the broken, useless engine. Dad got up to follow. Eager to stretch her legs, Sky opened her door too, but he told her, sharply, to get back in and wait.

In the dusty, airless back seat of the car, Chip was looking at pictures in a magazine he'd pulled out of a litter bin.

Sky watched her parents through the closed window. They'd moved some distance from the car and stood facing each other on the side of the road. Sky felt she was outside a shop window, unable to hear the sound, whilst watching two people arguing on a TV. Cautiously, she wound the window down a crack and began to catch some of her father's unlinked phrases.

". . . *we* could hitch a lift . . . on our own . . . too much luggage . . ."

An ache of doubt started to gnaw at the pit of Sky's stomach. She knew Dad didn't mean the battered, cardboard suitcases in the car boot. He was talking about Chip and her. They'd become luggage, excess luggage at that!

Sky leant back against the seat, struggling to keep her face blank of any expression, trying hard to look as if she wasn't eavesdropping and praying Chip wouldn't hear what they were saying in case he kicked up a fuss.

But Dad wasn't looking her way. Mum was the one who kept turning to point towards the children and Sky heard her say, ". . . can't abandon . . . just walk out . . . *our* kids."

After a while Dad angrily turned away and wandered off alone up the dusty road towards the city.

Mum came back to the car and sank into her seat.

Without looking up from his magazine Chip asked, "Where's Dad gone?"

"To get food," she said.

Chip instantly dropped his magazine and bounced about. "I want to go with him."

But Mum wouldn't let him. "You wait here with us," she said and he slumped back into his magazine, sulking.

Sky forced herself to ask Mum the one question she didn't really want to hear answered. "He *will* come back, won't he?"

"Of course he will," Mum said. She'd tried to sound reassuring but Sky noticed the answer came too quickly, so she knew Mum didn't believe the answer any more than she did.

While Dad was away Sky and Chip messed about in the field beside the road. Mum busied herself washing clothes in the stream, laying them out on the bank to dry in the sunshine. But each time she stood up, Mum shaded her eyes against the sun and peered down the long, straight road towards the city.

The car sat empty by the side of the dusty road, the

4

doors wide open, its bonnet still up. A huge, stranded, rusty, brown bird, wings outstretched, beak wide open, demanding food.

Dad did return that night. He brought a pizza, a bag of fruit and a litre bottle of Coke. Later, Mum and Dad climbed out of the car and had another row.

That was three nights back. Since when, he'd walked into the city every day to look for work and returned each evening with less and less to eat.

Last night they'd all shared a family pack of potato crisps and a can of Coke.

Just the memory of that sketchy meal brought hunger pangs back to Sky. "Mum," she murmured. There was no reply. She spoke a little louder the next time. "Mum, I'm hungry."

Mum was a light sleeper, so when she still didn't answer, Sky sat up and found there was nobody in either of the two front seats. Neither Mum nor Dad.

She checked the dashboard clock. It was a little after seven. Maybe they'd gone to find something for breakfast?

Sky's sudden movement had rocked the car's suspension. Chip stirred in his sleep. Sky froze. She didn't want to wake him yet, not until there was something to eat, though deep inside her she already knew her parents had gone for good.

She felt she ought to cry. If she hadn't seen this coming for days, she might have, but waiting had been the worst part. Watching whenever Mum or Dad left the car, wondering if this would be their final departure, only to have them come back behaving as if they'd never so much as considered leaving.

Sky tried to picture the actual moment of their going and found it easy to see her dad doing it, but not Mum.

He'd have just got out of the car, collected a few

5

things from the boot and walked off without a backward glance. Not that he'd always been like that. Sky could remember him playing games with her, singing songs even, but not after he'd lost his job and what little money they'd had drained away. Then Dad had quickly grown hard and bitter. Maybe that change happened because he was too frightened to face up to his real feelings; not daring to risk the smallest glance down whilst standing on the edge of his personal, dark chasm.

Even Mum had toughened up over those last few weeks. She wouldn't have been human if she hadn't, although it was she who'd held them together, tried to make life as normal as it could possibly be, living out of suitcases in a car. She'd always insisted they washed and cleaned their teeth. She gave the children more than half of her share of the food. When there was nothing for anyone to eat she'd hugged them, sung them to sleep stroking their hair.

How could she have gone? Maybe Dad had promised they'd come back as soon as they found something?

Sky was positive that Mum, as she left, would have glanced back, she just knew she would, but probably Dad would have dragged her away. Had *she* cried? Sky hoped so!

After an hour had passed, Sky could bear the silence no longer. She looked down at Chip, so small and skinny lying there, it seemed a shame to wake him.

Sky wondered why she shouldn't get out of the car too and walk off! She was ashamed to realise that she was tempted to, but why should she be saddled with the responsibility her parents wouldn't shoulder?

Chip was only six, he couldn't walk far. She was eleven and strong for her age.

Maybe, if it hadn't been for Chip, her parents would have taken her with them. Perhaps if he hadn't been so small, needing to be carried all the time, she'd have been with her mother at that very moment.

Sky realised the danger of such thoughts and pushed them away. "Chip! Wake up!"

Unlike his sister, Chip woke quickly. He opened his large, brown eyes; a shutter being thrown open to flood a room with sunlight. His lashes were long, like a girl's. Sky had the strong jaw, corn-coloured hair and deep blue eyes of her father.

"You'll never be a beauty," Mum always said, "but they'll never ignore you."

Chip's face was a miniature version of Mum's, it had the same delicate bones and the same "at-peace-with-the-world" look which concealed an unexpected strength of character. For a second Sky so much resented the close resemblance, she wanted to slap him for what Mum had done.

"Sky." He sighed her name by way of greeting, pleased to see her.

She wished she didn't have to break the news to him. She knew that what she was about to say would sound like a tease, but this time one that had gone badly wrong. "Chip," she spoke slowly so that he would understand, for Sky didn't think she would be able to bear repeating anything, "Mum and Dad have gone."

Chip looked puzzled. "Gone for food?"

Sky shook her head. "No, not this time. This time they've gone for good." She watched his face carefully. "You're not to cry. It's no good crying."

"I'm not going to," he said fiercely, but there was a tremor in his voice and he'd pursed his lips fiercely to stop them quivering.

She went on quickly. "There's nothing to cry about." She knew she had to add the next bit but,

7

much as she loved her brother, resented it. "I'll look after you."

Chip didn't cry. Instead he screamed and shouted, beating the seat with his fists. "I want my mum!"

He shouted it over and over again, drumming his feet against the door, banging his head against the window. In the confined space of the car the words were painfully loud. Sky wanted to cover her ears, blot out the noise and with it, the reality of what had happened to them.

But at least Chip's tantrum gave her something to do; doing was safer than thinking.

She grabbed his fists. "Stop it, Chip. Stop it! Shouting won't bring them back."

Slowly Chip calmed down, but his eyes smouldered angrily, convinced, as she had been about him that in some way which he couldn't fathom, this was really all Sky's fault. Or, at the very least, there was something she could have done to prevent it happening.

"It'll be a game, like playing house," she suggested brightly, but knowing her voice sounded as brittle as her mother's had when she'd assured Sky Dad was coming back.

Mention of a game seemed to please Chip, but Sky wasn't nearly so comfortable with the idea. She was old enough to realise that a game is something you can easily give up when it gets too much, or boring. This was very different; once started, this was a "game" from which there would be no escape.

Even before they'd set out to go to the City for food, Chip was already being a pest.

"I've got to take Ted with me." He grabbed the threadbare, one-eyed, stuffed toy off the back seat.

"There's no point!" Sky argued, tossing Ted into the back of the car. "We're only going to find something

8

to eat, then we'll be back. The less we have to carry the better."

But Chip's screams of protest forced her to compromise and she agreed to him taking a little, blue pick-up truck which would easily fit in his jeans pocket. Though, thinking that if she was forced to play the part of an adult she might as well talk like one, she warned him, "Don't expect me to look for it when you lose it!"

They were still in sight of the car when Chip first limped to a halt, moaning, "I've got a stone in my trainer."

"Well, take it out," Sky said testily.

Chip did as he was told and then looked up helplessly. "Will you tie them for me?"

"I could tie my own laces by the time I was six."

"So can I, but they keep coming undone again."

Sky was bending down, putting a double knot in the second lace, when a lorry passed them, kicking up a choking cloud of dust.

As the dust began to settle, Sky realised the lorry had pulled up alongside their car and two men were climbing out.

She broke into a run. "They're going to break into our car and steal everything."

"Wait for me!" Chip called out, scampering after her.

But it was far worse than Sky had thought. From behind the lorry's cab, one of the men was swinging a crane out over their car. "Oh, no! They can't do that!" she wailed, but the other man was already fixing chains which hung from the crane's hook around the car.

"What are they doing?" Chip asked, as he caught up.

"They think our car's been abandoned and they're hauling it away for scrap," Sky said.

9

"I've got to get Ted," Chip shouted and scooted off up the road.

"Never mind Ted," Sky said as she ran beside him, "everything we possess is locked in the boot of that car. All our clothes, everything!"

The car was already off the ground by the time they reached it.

Sky shrieked at the man on the ground. "That's our car, you can't take it!"

All he said was, "Clear off!"

But his mate on the lorry stopped the hoist and asked, "What's up?"

"This kid reckons this is her car," the first man laughed.

"It is," Sky protested.

"And it's got my Ted inside it," Chip added fiercely.

For a few seconds the car hung in mid-air, swinging slightly, suspended just above head height. The man beside the crane's controls looked uncertain, but the one on the ground insisted, "Let's get this crate on. We've still got two others to collect yet."

"All our stuff's in there!" Sky shrieked.

But the crane had started again and drowned her out, except for the man standing next to her. "I've already looked inside, there was nothing."

"In the boot!" Sky pulled at his arm, but the man threw her away, sending her sprawling in the dust.

"Clear off, before I clout you."

Tears streamed down Sky's face as she picked herself up and watched, helpless, as their car was lifted high up into the air and then dumped unceremoniously on the back of the truck.

And then, before she'd thought of scrambling up on to the truck to try and retrieve any of their belongings, the two men climbed into the cab and drove off.

For Sky, as well as providing them with shelter, the car had been a vital symbol. While it sat on the

10

side of the road she'd desperately clung to the possibility, no matter how remote, that her parents might come back. Now there was nowhere for them to come back to!

That truck was hauling away Sky's last hope.

Very quietly Chip shuffled up beside her and taking her hand he said, "My Ted was in there."

Unfairly, Sky expressed her own distress by shouting at Chip. "Never mind your Ted, that was our home! Now what do we do?"

Two

It took them hours to reach the outskirts of the city. No wonder Dad was away all day when he came, Sky thought, but at least he didn't have to bring Chip with him.

Chip dragged behind all the way, finding any excuse to stop. A particular favourite was constantly asking for drinks. Fortunately, before they'd set out, Sky had thought of filling the empty Coke bottle with water from the nearby stream.

Then he wanted to be carried. "Dad used to carry me on his shoulders," he grumbled when Sky refused.

"Well, Dad isn't here, is he?" she said harshly. "And you're far too heavy for me to carry you like that."

Only when Chip stopped moving altogether, gripped his stomach and started crying, "I've got cramp!", did Sky give in. For a while she struggled along giving him a piggyback.

Throughout the journey Sky worried about what food they might be able to buy with the few coins she'd managed to find. Having searched all over the car, in the glove compartment, under the rugs and down the backs of the seats, she'd only come up with a handful of change.

As they began to pass the first run-down houses, from their open doorways, ragged children younger than themselves stared, wide-eyed and silent, at Chip and Sky.

From beneath a derelict truck, from which most of

the vital parts had been removed to the extent that the carcase rested on four breeze blocks rather than wheels, two dogs leapt out, snarling and snapping at them.

For the hundredth time Chip complained, "I'm hungry!"

"There aren't any shops round here," she pointed out, "we'll be able to get something once we're properly in the city."

Chip's eyes widened. "Are you sure it'll be safe to go right in?"

"Don't be silly," she said, jerking his hand to persuade him to increase his sluggish footsteps.

But Chip braced himself like a dog resisting the tug of a lead. "Mum always said we shouldn't wander about in towns and cities without a grown-up."

Sky mimicked him. "Well, your mum isn't here and we haven't got a grown-up, have we? So you'll have to make do with me."

Chip obstinately thrust out his bottom lip. "What about the Catchers?"

The Catchers lurked in the dark corner of every child's imagination. Though their real title was "Child Protection Officers", the Catchers' work was so like dog-catchers that the name had stuck.

As the rich had got richer and the poor poorer, the Child Protection Units were hastily formed as part of the response to the public outcry about the numbers of vagrants living rough in the cities.

The Catchers' specific aim was to round up some of the vast and continually growing army of kids who'd taken to eking out a living on the streets.

Some, like Sky and Chip, had simply been abandoned. Others, as they grew older, had been turned out of their homes to fend for themselves by parents too poor to cope with feeding large families.

Forced to live by their wits, they mostly appeared

to exist as beggars, or petty criminals, sleeping rough in shop doorways, or any other meagre shelter they could find.

Though Catchers were not allowed to enter people's houses, there were few children of Chip's age who went to sleep without first checking under the bed for a Catcher. Last waking moments were often spent cowering under the bedclothes, imagining Catchers looming up from the shadows of their darkened bedrooms, eager to snatch up and carry off their victims. Too many unkind parents would threaten to give naughty children away to the Catchers.

In reality most people had never had anything to do with the Catchers, but that didn't stop all kinds of myths springing up around them, until it was very difficult, even for adults, to sort fact from ficton.

"That's all stories!" Sky said scornfully.

"No, it isn't. I've seen them!"

"Yes, everyone knows they exist," Sky agreed, "but they don't collect up children who *belong* to people."

"They caught my friend Bugs once."

"Yes, but his parents went and got him back. Like I said, they don't pick up kids who belong to somebody."

"And who do we belong to?" Chip's brown eyes searched Sky's face. "Who'd come to get us back?"

Sky had no answer to that, so instead she fell back on the old grown-up solution of changing the subject. "Are you hungry, or not?"

"Yes."

"Well, come on then!" But she could see the struggle still churning round in his mind, so she tried hard to sound reassuring. "Look, Chip, there's no food here and anyway, I think the Catchers mostly work at night. It'll be perfectly safe."

"I don't know," Chip said, doubtfully.

Sky knew that the longer they hung around, the

more likelihood there was of Chip's worst fears coming true. Their best chance was to look busy and keep moving. She searched round desperately. "Oh, look, I can see a stall up the road. Maybe we could buy a drink, or something.

Unimpressed, Chip said, sullenly, "We've got water."

"I mean a proper drink. Iced Cola?"

"I want an ice cream."

Sky knew blackmail when she heard it. But she also accepted that somehow she had to get Chip moving again. If the price of that was an ice cream, that's what she'd have to pay! "Come on then!"

Chip instantly leapt up, a coiled spring of energy suddenly released, and bounded down the dusty road. By the time Sky caught up, Chip was already standing on tip-toe, clinging on to the side of the stall with both hands, like someone trying to scale a wall, his nose pressed against the glass front. "A double scoop of strawberry with sauce and one of those chocolate things stuck in it."

Sky's heart sank when she read the chalked-up price list. "A drink would last longer," she suggested.

"You promised me ice cream."

"Okay!" And she ordered, "A small strawberry cornet, with no extras!"

"It's not fair," Chip grumbled.

Sky, who would have loved one too, said, "It's either that, or nothing."

Chip sank back on his heels. "Oh, all right."

The moment she'd handed over the coins, there were so few left in her pocket, Sky wished she'd never mentioned ice cream. But at least it had got Chip walking again, though the sun was so hot that, even before he'd taken his first lick, a thin trail of pink liquid was already trickling over his hand.

Sky looked on enviously. "Give us a lick."

15

"No, get one of your own."

Sky shrugged. He just didn't understand!

It was past midday when they reached the crowded streets of the city centre and Sky began to wonder if coming here had been such a good idea. She'd thought with more people around they wouldn't be so noticeable. She quickly realised that, having slept in their clothes, they stood out from the smartly dressed shoppers and business people like aliens from another planet.

She felt dwarfed by the towering office blocks and shabby outside the expensive shops whose owners' names, highlighted in gold, were carved into their marble fascias.

Even the gleaming limousines which swept along the broad avenues seemed to be of a totally different species to their departed, battered, brown car.

Aware of the curious stares they were attracting, even from a workman up a ladder attaching an election poster to one of the few vacant lampposts, Sky urged Chip on with constant prods.

"Can't we sit down for a bit, my feet hurt?" he pleaded.

Sky's did too. "No," she insisted, "we've got to keep moving until we find some food."

"But there's plenty of food," Chip said, pointing at the surrounding shops, all of which had huge displays of every kind, from potato crisps and vegetables, to chocolates, or huge joints of meat.

Sky shook her head. "Don't argue. They're all too expensive. Let's see if we can find some kind of market."

She was so busy, searching round every street corner for stalls, that she failed to notice what was heading straight for her.

Chip clutched her arm. "Look!"

Cruising slowly towards them was a big black van with huge chrome bumpers like cowcatchers. On a bar above the cab was a battery of spotlights and on the cab doors, in white letters beneath the city coat of arms, were the words "Child Protection Unit".

Both men in the cab wore dark blue shirts with broad epaulettes on the shoulders. Their eyes were hidden by sunglasses and they wore black caps with silver badges and shiny peaks.

Chip froze as he hissed, "It's the Catchers."

Three

"Come on!" Sky tried to move Chip away.

But Chip just stared at the approaching van. "You said the Catchers weren't out in the daytime."

Sky tugged harder, trying to get him into a nearby entry. "They won't even notice us if we go down here."

But Chip appeared to be glued to the spot; a rabbit fascinated by a weaving snake.

Positive they'd been spotted, the van was only metres away, she picked Chip up bodily and heaved him into the alley like a sack.

The shock of being picked up and dropped seemed to kick-start Chip back into action and he ran.

They ran down narrow twisting alleys, bumping into people and tripping over kerbs. At last, completely out of breath, they sank on to the steps of a block of offices.

Before Sky even had time to recover, Chip was already crying. "I want my mum," he sobbed.

Sky felt the same way, but this was no time for thoughts of that kind. "You've got ice cream all round your mouth," she said, wrapping an old tissue round her finger and sticking it under Chip's nose. "Lick!"

Still snivelling, Chip obeyed, pulling a face as Sky tried to clean up his runny nose which had mixed with ice cream to form a crust of gunge around his upper lip. "It's no good crying," she said firmly. "Let's just get some food and get out of here as fast as we can." She pointed at a row of stalls just across the street. "That looks more like it."

Chip trailed behind while Sky looked to see what the stalls offered. There were several selling fruit, another piled with loaves of bread and cakes, and one, surrounded by huge flies, displayed joints of gristly meat.

"The trouble is they don't show any prices," Sky mumbled as she tried to decide how best to spend their money. She bought two buns and with only one silver coin left, moved to a fruit stall. The stallholder, a fat, unshaven man whose arms and shoulders overflowed from a grubby vest, eyed them suspiciously.

"How much are bananas?" Sky asked.

"Two for twenty," he said, without removing the chewed cigarillo from his thick lips.

"I'll have two, please."

Without a word he took the coin from Sky and deliberately handed her two small, overripe bananas from the very back of the stall.

Sky wished she'd taken two of the better ones off the front, but lacked the courage to argue. She merely held out her hand for the change.

The man looked surprised. "Yes? What do you want?"

"My change, please."

"There isn't any. You gave me twenty."

"Fifty," Sky insisted timidly.

The man snatched out the cigarillo and leant over the stall, thrusting his sweaty, angry face at Sky. "You calling me a liar?"

"It *was* a fifty." Sky, embarrassed, outraged and upset at the thought of being swindled out of the last of their money, was close to tears.

But the greengrocer waved her away. "Clear off, before I call the police."

"Not until I've got my change."

Other stallholders, who hadn't heard the earlier part of the conversation, turned to listen.

Playing up to them, the man raised his voice. "Change? You haven't even paid me for those two bananas yet," the man lied. He lunged at Sky, trying to snatch back the fruit and when she instinctively jumped back out of reach, he shouted at the top of his voice, "Stop thief!"

Sky knew when she was beaten. Trying to clutch the bananas and buns to her with one arm while grabbing hold of Chip with her free hand, they fled.

Shouts from the stallholders, as they gave chase, ricocheted off the walls of the narrow street.

One of the precious bananas slipped out of Sky's grip and was pulped beneath their feet. A bread roll jumped out of the bag and bounced off across the road into the gutter, but there was no time to recover it.

They'd almost reached the corner when a big black van pulled to a halt at the end of the street, completely blocking their escape. Two Catchers climbed slowly down from the cab and waited, arms folded, for Sky and Chip to arrive and give themselves up.

Sky pulled Chip to a halt. They were trapped. Going back would bring them face to face with the angry stallholders, going forwards would inevitably mean being scooped up by the Catchers.

"This way!"

Sky turned. On the opposite side of the street was a skinny boy dressed in grubby, torn jeans and a brown jumper, riddled with holes, through which tufts of tartan shirt appeared. He was waving frantically, urging Sky towards a gap he'd created by swinging back two loose boards in a wooden fence.

Caught between the angry stallholders and the Catchers, Sky knew there was no choice but to trust the boy. The greengrocer, still yelling, was only a few

20

strides away as Sky helped Chip through the gap and followed him.

The moment the boy swung the planks back into position and wedged them securely, angry fists hammered on the fence.

"Welcome to the Jungle," the boy said with a brief grin.

They were on a long, narrow patch of waste ground, overgrown with head-high weeds, which was sandwiched between two rows of tall, derelict houses. Sky only had the briefest glimpse of her new surroundings before the boy dived down into what looked like the mouth of a tunnel which had been hacked through the undergrowth.

"Follow me," he called over his shoulder.

Sky bent double and darted after him. If she hadn't had to keep waiting for Chip, Sky would have had no difficulty in keeping up, but Chip, with his short legs, kept tripping over the tangle of roots and branches beneath his feet.

They fell back further and further, until there was no sound, or sign, of the swiftly moving boy and Sky began to think they might be lost for ever amongst the dense mass of vegetation.

Then, as they came out into a clearing in the middle of the waste ground, they found the boy squatting down on the grass, waiting for them. "They'll never follow us out here," he grinned breathlessly. "You okay? I thought I'd lost you for a minute."

"I'm fine, it's my brother who can't keep up," Sky said, jerking Chip's hand.

"He did better than I would at his age," the boy said, earning a grateful, but shy, smile from Chip. "I'm Dig." He was a little older than Sky and had lively brown eyes under a thick mop of black hair.

"I'm Sky and this is Chip."

"You certainly made yourselves a few new friends

back there!" Dig observed, plucking a strand of grass and chewing its end.

"That greengrocer accused me of stealing," Sky explained, "but he was the thief. He took my money, wouldn't give me any change and then swore I'd never paid at all."

The boy shrugged. "Happens all the time. Bad luck the Catchers turning up when they did though." Dig looked more closely at the two of them. "You're new around here, aren't you?"

Grateful as she was to Dig for rescuing them from the Catchers, he was still a stranger and Sky didn't want to tell him everything. Lately Dad had cautioned them, "Keep a close mouth on your troubles, people only take advantage. When you're down, most people just want to push you down further."

"Yes," she said, "we only came into town for food." Which was true as far as it went.

But before she could stop him, Chip piped up, "Our mum and dad have gone away and left us."

"Oh, I see. Haven't you got any relatives you could go to?"

Sky shook her head. "Dad had a row with his family years ago, so I don't even know where they live. Mum was an only child and her parents are both dead."

"Then you'll be looking for the Tip."

"What tip?"

"That's where most of the street kids, Throwaways like us, live. The Catchers don't bother us much out there. They only pick us up when we come into the city, where the posh people can see us."

Sky felt Throwaways was an exact description of herself. Her only plan, to find something to eat and return to the car, had come to nothing now that all their money and the car had disappeared. The frights she'd had as they'd wandered around, lost in the unfamiliar city, had deeply undermined her usual self-confidence.

After two narrow escapes from the Catchers, she would gladly have stayed hidden in the Jungle forever, but she knew that wasn't possible. At least, if she agreed to go to the Tip, she'd be able to rely on Dig's knowledge of the city and his protection.

Chip broke through her thoughts. "I'm hungry."

Sky skinned the only banana she'd managed to hold on to, squashed it more than broke it into two and handed half over to Chip. She was about to eat the other half herself, when she noticed the way Dig was watching her. After all, she thought, they would never have escaped from the Catchers without his help. "Dig, you eat this, I'll have the bread roll."

"Are you sure?" Dig asked politely, but almost before she had a chance to nod, he'd stuffed the whole piece in his mouth.

Sky's roll turned out to be stale and it was only while her mouth was clogged up with dry crumbs that she realised that while she was cleaning up Chip's face she'd put the water bottle down on the office steps and forgotten it.

"What do you mean by the Tip?" she asked.

"It's a rubbish tip."

Chip's eyebrows shot up in wide-eyed admiration. "You live on a rubbish tip?"

"Yes, I'm a Picker," Dig said proudly, but when Sky looked blank he explained, "I make a living from the stuff I find on the Tip. I don't live on it though, but in the shanty town the street kids have built just next to it."

"We've got nowhere to live," Sky admitted, "but I don't see how we'd be any better off at the Tip."

"With nowhere to live you could hardly be *worse* off, could you?" Dig grinned as if such things were everyday occurrences in his life. "You're welcome to come and share my place for a while."

As things were, Sky couldn't see there was any choice. She certainly wasn't keen on the idea of living beside a rubbish dump, but they had to have somewhere to sleep, preferably safe from the Catchers. "Thanks," she said.

Dig smiled. "You're welcome."

Sky stood up. "Shall we go?"

But Dig lay back in the grass. "Not yet. The Catchers will be swarming around out there like flies, still looking for you two. We'll leave it a while until it starts to go dark."

The sun was setting as Dig led them round thick tangles of briar and skirted patches of stinging nettles until they reached the edge of the Jungle. They stopped in the long evening shadows cast by one of the big, old houses. "We can get out through here."

"Do you think we should?" Sky asked. "Somebody might live here."

Dig laughed. "Are you crazy? Look at the place!"

Most of its grimy windows had been broken and the back door swung crazily from one hinge.

Old tin cans and paper littered the yard. The inside of the house was filled with the sickening smell of cat droppings and human excrement.

As they made their way along a gloomy hall towards the front door, a carpet of broken glass crunched loudly on the tiles beneath their feet. Beside them the remains of a rickety staircase led to the floor above. Most of its wooden banister rails had been taken for firewood.

They were halfway to the open door when two hands shot out from a dark corner beneath the stairs and caught Sky and Chip in an iron grip.

Four

Sky and Chip both yelled as a filthy old man, dressed in rags, thrust his face up close. His thinning, grey hair was matted to his head, his pale blue eyes were watery and bloodshot and stale wine soured his breath. "What you doing in 'ere?" he demanded through stained and broken teeth.

Chip continued to scream, struggling and kicking as he tried to free himself.

"We didn't know there was anyone in here," Sky stammered.

Dig walked quickly back and immediately took command.

"Don't worry, Chip, he may look horrible but he's harmless. Let them go, Horsemeat. They're all right, they're with me."

The old man scowled, but didn't release them. "Think you can come through 'ere whenever you like, don't you?" he grumbled. "Disturbing a man's rest."

Dig took no notice. "We've got as much right to be here as you. Let them go."

"Not so fast," Horsemeat leered. "Got any money?"

Chip blurted out, "She has."

"Shut up, stupid!" Sky hissed, but it was too late.

Horsemeat released Chip, who ran to join Dig, and used both hands to twist his grip of Sky's tee shirt even tighter, until it almost choked her. "'And it over, little girl, before you get 'urt!"

25

"He's lying," Sky said hoarsely. "I've no money left."

"I don't believe you. 'And it over!"

"I've spent it all," Sky coughed. She was going very red in the face.

Dig swiftly pulled one of the few remaining rails out from the broken banisters and threatened Horsemeat with it. "I've warned you!"

Still hanging on to Sky, Horsemeat reached behind him with his free hand. Gripping it by the neck, he produced an empty wine bottle. He smashed it against the cupboard door and thrust the jagged edge up near to Sky's face. "You come near me and she gets it!"

But Dig didn't hesitate. He brought down the banister rail smartly, right on Horsemeat's wrist. As Horsemeat howled with pain and dropped the bottle, his grip on Sky loosened and she was able to pull free.

"Don't come back, if you know what's good for you!" Horsemeat bellowed after them as they ran down the hall, out through the front door and into the street.

Sky, still recovering from her fright, was furious that Dig, the very person she relied upon for protection, had immediately led them into the danger. "I thought you said nobody lived there?"

Dig shrugged it off. "Can't always tell, still no harm done."

"No harm? I nearly got murdered in there!" she hollered at him and then turned on Chip. "And as for you! Why did you say I'd got money when you knew I hadn't."

"Sky, the kid was scared," Dig said quietly. "Calm down, you're both all right, that's the main thing."

By the time they reached the city centre darkness had fallen. Chip was hungry, worn out and fratchy.

"When are we going to eat?" he moaned. "I've got stomach ache."

"Soon," Dig promised.

The brightly lit shop windows attracted Sky's attention even more than they had during the day. Perhaps it was because she had lost all her own possessions that the displays of rich dresses, glittering jewellery and highly polished furniture seemed to belong to a totally different world to the one in which she lived. She couldn't resist a wry smile when she read the price tag on one dress, a frothy confection of wild silk edged with silver. The money somebody would spend buying that would feed them all for at least a month!

Dig stopped outside a fast-food restaurant.

Chip pressed his nose against the windows, his eyes almost eating the food off the diners' paper plates. Hardly able to tear himself away from the sight, he asked Dig, "Is this where we're going to eat?"

To Sky's surprise Dig nodded, but as Chip ran towards the open doors Dig hauled him back. "Not inside! There's nearly as much food out here."

Everything became clear as Dig fought through the cloud of wasps and flies and scared off a mangy dog before plunging his hands deep into the contents of the pavement litter bin. It was anchored to a lamppost, just beneath another election poster which, Sky couldn't help noticing, carried the portrait of a very well-fed-looking candidate.

"Don't just stand there," Dig said, passing her a pile of take-away food containers, "you look too!"

Hungry as she was, Sky felt sick. Reluctantly, one by one she opened the boxes. They were all so light she hoped they might be empty, but one contained a handful of french fries and a half-eaten hamburger together with some cigarette ash, a plastic knife and fork and an empty sauce sachet. The cold, congealed food appeared to have been mashed together with a liberal helping of tomato sauce.

"Yuck!" Sky said.

She was about to toss the box back when Dig stopped her. "Don't waste it!"

"I can't eat that!" Sky said, her nose wrinkling with disgust.

"I will," Chip offered, greedily snatching the box from her hand.

Sky took it back. "Chip, you can't! You never know who's been eating from it."

"I don't care either," Chip said grabbing the container. "I'm starving!"

"But it's probably covered in germs. You can still see the tooth marks in that hamburger bun!" Sky shuddered.

"Then I'll eat from the other side," Chip mumbled through a moustache of french fries which dangled from his rapidly moving mouth.

"You can't afford to be choosy," Dig pointed out as he offered her the choice of some chicken nuggets, or a remnant of breaded fish.

Though her stomach heaved, she was about to put the chicken in her mouth when an older boy in a smart uniform ran out shouting, "Clear off, before I call the Catchers!"

They ran and the chicken nugget Sky dropped was gratefully snapped up by the mangy mongrel.

Their next stop was at a street market which was closing down for the night. Sky and Chip watched as Dig produced a carrier bag from his jeans pocket. He darted swiftly between the departing barrows and fought off the streetsweeper's brushes to pick up discarded fruit and vegetables which had fallen on the street.

"Half that stuff's rotten!" Sky said scornfully.

Dig proudly polished a severely bruised apple on the sleeve of his jersey and tossed it to her. "Then eat the half that isn't!"

Sky was still savouring her first bite when Dig urgently hissed, "The Catchers again!"

As the black van cruised slowly down the street, a hand-operated searchlight swept across the pavements and doorways on either side.

Dig spotted a gate which opened on to some stone steps that led down to the shadowy basement area outside a house. "Down there!"

Stumbling and tripping down the steps, Dig and Sky half-carried Chip between them.

"Down behind the dustbins!" Dig said.

The Catchers' searchlight passed over their heads as they squatted, barely hidden, behind the smelly bins. The vehicle pulled up right outside the gate so close that, through its open windows, they could hear the static hissing on the radio and even some of the Catchers' conversation.

"I'm positive I saw some kids heading this way."

The one nearest the kerb, who was leaning out of the window, calmly replied, "I didn't see a thing."

"Mainly because you don't want to, Spindor," the first man said. "Sometimes I think you're too soft for this job."

"No, I'm not," Spindor said. "I just didn't see what you thought you saw, Shakey."

Sky peered cautiously round the edge of the bin and found herself looking straight into the deep brown eyes of the Catcher called Spindor. There was no doubt in Sky's mind as she ducked down, her heart beating fast, that he'd had a clear view of her.

But the strange thing was that, instead of him leaping out of the van to scoop her up, Sky heard him say to his partner, "I'm telling you, Shakey, there's nobody down there."

29

"Maybe we ought to take a proper look," Shakey suggested.

At that moment, in the house behind the children, a light was switched on in the basement room. Its yellow light spilled out into the tiny courtyard, projecting the exaggerated shadow of a woman walking towards the window.

"Get right down!" Dig said.

"I can't get any lower, there isn't room," Sky whispered back.

The woman was about to close the curtains when she caught sight of the three children crouched down in her yard and froze.

"Damn!" Dig whispered. "She's spotted us."

"She's bound to give us away," Sky muttered.

But just as Sky thought the game was up, the Catchers' radio burst into life and although she couldn't catch what was said, to her immense relief, she heard Spindor saying, "Unit 6, that's us. Better move it!" The van's engine was thrown into gear and it roared off.

The woman in the window glanced up briefly at the back of the departing black van, but did nothing to attract the Catchers' attention. Instead, giving the children a pitying shake of her head, she closed the curtains and moments later the light was switched off.

"That was too close," Dig said. "We'd better get out, fast!"

Sky couldn't understand why, when Spindor had seen her, he'd done nothing about it, but she kept quiet all the same. She was beginning to worry that far from keeping them out of trouble, Dig kept leading them into more.

Dig led the way swiftly through the outskirts of the city, passing through dingy houses and finally factories. They crossed over the tracks of a big railway sidings where grumbling diesel engines noisily shunted trucks.

Eventually they came to a high, chain-link fence anchored to concrete posts. Strands of rusty barbed wire ran along the top. The wide gates were shut and held together by a heavy chain with a padlock on the inside.

Beside them was a small wooden hut from which hung a single naked bulb. By its light they saw a fat man who wore his broad-brimmed hat tipped back on his head. A leather gun holster hung from his belt, a belt almost hidden by the sheer size of the man's paunch. The chair he sat on was tilted back, front legs off the ground, its back resting against the lapboards of the hut as he sat, gazing into space.

Lying in the dust beside the man was a huge, black guard-dog which raised its head and pricked up its ears as they approached.

The combined smell of refuse, hot ashes and decay told Sky that they'd arrived at the Tip. Sky whispered to Dig, "Why do they pay a man to guard rubbish?"

Dig laughed. "They don't. He's here to stop illegal tipping. Everyone except the city authorities has to pay."

The dog growled and the night watchman swung the brilliant beam of a huge torch in their direction as he snapped, "Who's there?"

Shielding his eyes with his arm, Dig called back, "It's only me, Dig!"

The dog leapt forward, barking furiously, desperate to get at Dig, but frustrated by the fence.

"Going to get yourself hurt one day, boy, creeping up on people!" The man whistled the dog, which ignored him and kept barking and crashing against the fence. "Come here, you black-hearted devil!"

Still the dog took no notice, until the man reluctantly got off his chair and clouted it across the back with a thick truncheon. The dog yelped. "Then come when I call, you hear?" The man stayed by the fence. He pulled a single, crumpled cigarette from his shirt pocket and lit it with a match which he struck with his thumbnail. "So who's that with you?"

"Just a couple of new friends."

"You'd best get on your way, boy."

"Good night, Fingers."

The light moved away and then suddenly swung back. "Hey, Dig! You seen anything of Babe?"

Dig shook his head. "Not lately."

"If you do, tell her I was asking. Tell her she should come up here again sometime soon."

"I'll do that, Fingers! Night!"

With only moonlight to help them Dig led them single file, with Chip in the middle, down a narrow, worn path alongside the fence. "Fingers only works at night, but you want to watch out for him. He's not a very nice guy. Some of the kids think he's a paid police informer. I don't know if that's true, but he's always being nosy, so I tell him nothing."

Sky asked, "Who's Babe?"

"One of the girls who lived at the Tip."

"Where's she gone?"

"How should I know? Sky, life here isn't like life on the outside. In here things have beginnings, but they don't necessarily have a middle and an end. Somebody arrives, like you two now. They might mean a lot in your life and yet next day they'll be gone, you'll probably never see them again. Tomorrow you could go up to look for food and get picked up by the Catchers, or knocked down by a bus. Or maybe something good would come up for you. A job, or something. You wouldn't risk losing that just to come back and tell us. So on the Tip we'd probably never get to hear what happened to you. As far as we're concerned you'd just have disappeared. Some day you might pop back but you'd more than likely simply forget all about us. I'm sure I would," Dig said thoughtfully, "because this is a place to forget."

Trying to make conversation, Sky asked, "Why is Fingers so keen for Babe to go back up there?"

Dig stopped dead and turned back to Sky. "Another thing you ought to know about the Tip; people don't like people who pry into other people's business."

"Sorry."

"They'll tell you what they think you should know. Like you did with me. We've all got things we'd rather not talk about, okay?"

Sky nodded and they walked on until they came to a corner where the fence turned and disappeared steeply down into the darkness.

Below them, Sky saw the hundreds of tiny, flickering lights of the shanty town which clung to the sloping hillside and thought she could hear the distant sound of the sea.

"Nearly home now," Dig called over his shoulder.

Five

They soon found themselves moving between row after row of primitive shelters. Some, so far as Sky could see, were made from nothing more substantial than cardboard boxes. Most leaned heavily on their neighbours for support giving the impression that if one should collapse, all the others would go down like a run of dominoes.

One had a piece of old carpet slung over it for extra protection from the weather. Another consisted solely of a single sheet of rusty, corrugated iron, bent over to form a long, low tunnel. There were also several tents, patchwork quilts of rags and plastic bags, thrown over flimsy frames.

Many of the homes were lit with candles, or oil lamps, by whose pale, flickering light Sky made out shadowy figures moving around inside.

To Sky the place seemed like a cross between an ant hill and a rabbit warren. Over it all hung the hot, sour smell of the Tip and the sound of stray dogs, barking as they fought over scraps of food.

Even Sky, who'd lived in a car, had never in her worst imaginings thought of people existing in such pitiful conditions.

How they existed was beyond her experience or understanding, but her own misgivings about going there were rapidly increasing. What kind of hole did Dig live in? Most of the huts she'd seen were only fit for animals and barely large enough for one person, certainly not three.

As they passed through row after row of huts, Sky had the uncomfortable feeling of being watched with suspicion, if not hostility, by hundreds of pairs of unseen eyes. Her impression was confirmed when voices began to call out to Dig through the darkness.

"How's your luck, Dig?"

"Not as good as yours, Childie."

"Dig, how did you make out?"

"Got sidetracked, Boots, didn't do so well today."

"Who's that with you, Dig?"

"A couple of new friends, Buzz, so spread the word. They're called Sky and Chip and they're staying with me for a couple of days while they sort themselves out."

"They look hungry, Dig. It's no good coming to me . . ."

"Don't worry, Guts!" Dig laughed.

Only one person came for a proper look at the newcomers. She was a girl of about Sky's age, whose top half bulged out of a grubby white singlet. Below that she wore an absurdly short, red, satin skirt, smothered in dark stains. She tottered out unsteadily on a pair of scuffed, white, very high-heeled shoes.

The eyes with which the girl frankly examined Sky were heavily lined in black and lids bruised green with eye shadow. The girl tossed back her long, dark, greasy hair and said scathingly, "Dig! I'd have thought you could have found one with more meat on than that!"

Sky blushed with annoyance, but Dig smiled. "Sky, meet Cherry."

"Hi," said Cherry. "If you're looking for work, come and see me. Some men do like 'em skinny."

"Thanks," Sky said bleakly, not knowing what Cherry was talking about.

"Fingers was asking after Babe," Dig said. "Have you seen anything of her?"

Cherry shook her head. "Not this week and anyway, I don't suppose she'd go near Fingers again, not after what he did to her last time."

After they'd moved on Sky asked, "What did Cherry mean about work?"

"Don't ask!" Dig said and shuddered.

"But we're going to need money and if . . ."

Dig stopped and faced Sky. "Believe me, money isn't easy to come by around here, but there are pleasanter ways to get it than Cherry's." Sky still looked puzzled until Dig added bluntly, "Cherry sells herself to men, all right? Men who prefer spring chicken to old hen!"

"Oh, I see," Sky said, blushing and feeling foolish.

As they moved on, Chip sidled up to Sky and whispered, his voice heavy with distaste, "Why do men want to buy *her*?"

"Shut up, Chip," Sky hissed back, "you're too young to understand."

"Here we are, home!" Dig announced.

They were standing outside what to Sky looked like an old, wooden, hen house, but at least it was a little larger than some of the other huts.

"I'd better go in first and fix some light." Dig disappeared and returned with a lit candle stuck on to the upturned lid of a coffee jar. "Come inside."

Still fearing the worst, Sky ducked her head and entered Dig's home.

"Not bad," Sky said, glancing uncertainly round the tiny space. She and Dig both had to crouch slightly to avoid banging their heads on the low roof.

"It's built out of wood from old pallets," Dig proudly explained. "I didn't do it. The guy who lived here before me, Moonface, he put it together. We shared for a while when I first arrived and he always said I could have it if he left."

"It's got windows," Chip said.

The tiny size of the ragged scraps of material tacked up over windows reminded Sky of a Wendy house a friend had been given one Christmas.

Dig pulled back a curtain to show there wasn't glass behind it, but bars. "The bars were my idea. They let air in, but keep thieves out. They're two old footscrapers I found on the Tip."

The whole place was little more than two metres square. Half of that was occupied by a makeshift bed made from planks nailed at each corner to wooden crates which held it up off the ground. Thrown over it was a moth-eaten, but colourful blanket. "Are you sure there's going to room in here for all three of us?" Sky asked.

"There were four of you sleeping in your car!" Dig pointed out. "If we all sit down this won't feel so small."

Sky squatted on an upturned Coca Cola crate which had been padded with cloth to make it more comfortable.

Dig set the candle down on an old coffee table and joined Chip, who'd collapsed on to the bed.

"The mattress is made from some old sacks I sewed together with string. I pack them with screwed-up newspaper," Dig explained. "How about some tea?"

Sky, who was already regretting losing the chicken nugget and turning up her nose at the remains of the hamburger, nodded.

"I'd better get some fresh water," Dig said, picking up an empty, litre-sized, plastic bottle and heading for the door.

"Can I go for you?" Sky offered. "Where do you get it?"

"Thanks, but I'll get it. It comes from a standpipe and it's a bit tricky to find in the dark. I'll show you where everything is tomorrow."

37

As soon as Dig had gone Chip asked, "Where are we going to sleep?"

He looked so weary, Sky thought he might pass out any minute. "I don't know, on the floor, I guess."

Chip nodded happily. Sky could see that he was quite content with his surroundings. Then she remembered, he'd pestered Dad for ages to build him a tree house in the big, old tree that stood in the corner of their garden. This was probably something like he'd had in mind.

Sky saw it in a quite different way. For her this was just one further, painful step away from their old home and down a ladder which seemed doomed to end in absolute squalor and humiliation. Grateful as she was to have found shelter, and kind as Dig was in his own, rough way, to share what little he had, she could barely see herself spending more than one night in his primitive hut.

Although she had to admit he'd done his best to brighten the place up. The rough planks of all four walls were almost hidden by pictures. Some were old posters, others photographs from calendars, or bits torn out of magazines. But they all had two things in common. First, they were all country scenes; forests, fields of crops, animals grazing, or sweeping views, like the one of a deep valley with a sparkling river running through it. Sky also noticed there were no people in any of them.

Later, when Dig returned with the bottle of water, Chip was already asleep and snoring, curled up on one end of the bed, while Sky sat cross-legged on a length of scruffy red carpet laid across the dirt floor.

Pointing at the pictures, Sky asked politely, as if she were visiting relatives, "Were you brought up in the country?"

"Me?" Dig smiled. "No, but I'd love to live out there," Dig sighed as his eyes roved lovingly over the

38

pictures. "A couple of times I visited an uncle of mine who lived in a little village, I can't remember the name of it, but they were the best times I ever had."

"Why don't you have any pictures of people on your walls? Not even footballers, or pop stars."

Dig shrugged. "I've never thought about it."

"Only places and animals."

Dig looked steadily at Sky for a moment before he replied. "Well, places and animals can't hurt you, can they? I mean, what good have people ever done you? They only let you down in the end."

A day earlier Sky might have argued, but now she found it more difficult. "I suppose you're right."

He poured a little water into a smoke-blackened can and balanced it on some bricks which stood upended on the ground beside an old, battered metal chest. Inside the bricks was another tin. This one was closed and a length of teased out string came up through a hole in the lid to provide a wick. Once lit it burned weakly with a smoky, yellow flame.

Dig took two chipped mugs out of a cupboard that hung on the wall and got some part-used tea bags from another, which had a wire-mesh front and which he called his food store, though there was little in it;

But by the time he turned back, Sky too had fallen asleep, curled up on the carpet.

Dig grinned, pinched out the light under the kettle, dropped the blanket over Sky and then, pulling off his scruffy trainers, lay on the bed beside Chip before blowing out the candle.

Just as he was drifting off to sleep, he heard Sky stir in her sleep. "Mum!" she said softly.

"I know how you feel, kid!" Dig whispered. "But it takes more than wishing to bring them back again!"

In the distance a lone dog began to howl at the golden moon.

Six

Sky was the first to wake the following morning. She lay there, in unfamiliar surroundings, listening to the boys' steady breathing. She was cold and stiff after an uncomfortable, restless night on Dig's floor. Her mouth was horribly dry. Running her tongue round her furred-up teeth reminded her of her toothbrush and all their other possessions which had been hauled away with their old car.

Although Sky knew she ought to be worrying about essential items like their clothes, which they'd never have the money to replace, at that particular moment it was the loss of small personal things which hurt most. Losing those was like losing part of herself.

There was the shiny-backed hairbrush she'd been given for her ninth birthday and a mouth organ which she loved dearly, even though she hadn't played it for years. Also, tucked away under her clothes at the very bottom of the case, was a photograph of the whole family. It had been taken at the beach a few weeks before Dad lost his job.

If I'm never going to see them again, Sky thought, it would have been nice to have kept that.

She wondered where Mum and Dad had slept last night. Had they been lucky enough to meet someone who could help them like Dig?

Thinking of her mother, it occurred to Sky that now she was gone, there were so many things which had suddenly become part of a personal history which only she knew. Like most children, she'd always loved stories which began, "Do you remember when you . . .?"

Now some of her past had disappeared for ever with her parents. As Chip was younger there was nobody left with whom she could check her earliest memories to see if they were real or imaginary.

Worse, tears began to well up in her eyes when Sky found that the harder she struggled to fix a clear picture of Mum in her mind's eye, the more the image insisted on fading. Rather like the recurring dream she'd kept waking from during the night.

In it she'd been safely back in their old home. Chip and her father appeared clearly, but her mother, the person Sky most wanted to see, remained just out of sight. Over and over again Sky had tried, but no matter how much she turned her head, she never managed to see her mother.

"And this is after only one day!" she thought. "How long will it be before I won't be able to remember her at all?"

To dismiss those unpleasant thoughts Sky jumped up, lit the wick under the water can and pushed aside one of the curtains.

Through the barred window Sky found herself looking out across the stepped roofs of the shanties as they disappeared down the hill to meet the rocky coastline of a grey-green sea.

High above her and to the right, a digger, surrounded by flocks of hungry, noisy gulls and crows, was roughly ploughing through mountains of rubbish. Though it was still early, dotted about the slopes, dodging the falling waste, Sky could see scores of Pickers.

The sunshine on Chip's face woke him. After a brief look of confusion, he realised where he was and

41

stretched. "I'm going to look on the Tip for a new Ted today!" he said with a broad grin.

"If only that was *all* we had to do!" Sky thought.

Over extremely weak tea with no milk or sugar, Dig asked Sky what she planned to do. "I mean, you're welcome to stay for a while, but yesterday you didn't seem so keen."

Sky was uncomfortably aware of the two boys looking at her, particularly Chip, expecting some kind of decision. They could move on, fine, but where to? "I thought . . ." she began but stopped abruptly.

Dig came to her rescue. "Look, Sky, I know it isn't easy. A lot's happened to you and it'll take a while to sort everything out. Maybe you need to talk to some other people, find out how they've coped."

Sky raised an eyebrow. "Girls like Cherry?"

Dig smiled and shook his head. "No, I was thinking more of Berry."

"Who's she?"

"One of the Street-mothers. They look out for the very young kids who get left on their own. Suppose, some time, you had to leave Chip alone here . . ."

Sky cut in. "I wouldn't do that! I wouldn't walk out on Chip."

"I don't mean for good, but suppose you *had* to go somewhere. You could go knowing Chip was in safe hands if he was with someone like Berry."

"I'd rather stick with you, or Sky," Chip said.

"Of course you would," Dig agreed, "but I move around a lot and that can sometimes be dangerous, like yesterday!"

"I wouldn't be frightened to stay here on my own," Chip said, but Sky knew he wasn't as brave and confident as he was trying to sound.

Besides, Dig wouldn't entertain that idea. "The Tip's an odd place. Most of the people here live by

42

some sort of code, but there are lunatics everywhere and you'd be far safer staying with Berry."

"Doesn't Berry have to work too?" Sky asked.

Dig shook his head. "People pay her with food and stuff for looking after their kids. Come on," Dig jumped up, "I'll show you round and we'll probably meet her at the same time."

Sky was quite surprised to discover that the shanty-town, far from being the shapeless mass she'd imagined the previous night, turned out to be much more like a real town, though on a smaller, less permanent scale.

Most of the houses were properly arranged in streets. As they walked along the dusty paths between them Sky was aware, as she had been the night before, that both she and Chip were being examined by everyone they passed. Sky was beginning to feel as if she was constantly on trial, judged in some silent way, but whenever she caught them looking, their eyes would swivel swiftly away.

Near the centre of the camp was an open space of beaten earth.

"This is where people usually meet for a chat," Dig explained. "We use this pole as a notice board, where people can stick up bits of news and swaps."

Sky glanced at some of the scraps of paper. *Stay away from Tooley Street – Catchers are having a sweep. Buzz. Anyone got a saw I can borrow for a couple of days? Road Runner.*

"If there's some sort of emergency you beat on that drum and everyone comes running." Dig pointed to the sawn-off base of an oil drum which hung by a length of rope from the pole. The indentations on the drum's face had been decorated with a geometric pattern in white and red.

Beneath the drum, children were collecting water

in bottles and buckets, or washing themselves under a running tap.

"That's the standpipe where I came last night to get the water. It's the only safe water on the place but even that ought to be boiled before drinking."

"How come you've got water laid on?"

"We haven't," Dig grinned. "At least I don't think any of the Outsiders know we have. It's tapped out of the supply to the watchmen's hut, you remember, where you met Fingers?" Sky nodded. "At first it only came as far as the top of the camp, but the camp got bigger and so each time somebody found another length of hose pipe it was brought further down the hill. Oh, and the lavatories are in that block of huts on the end."

Sky couldn't believe her ears. "Lavatories?!"

"Sure. Doing it anywhere else is one of the few things you can be thrown off the site for. There's enough illness and disease around here without spreading it. We've only got buckets with makeshift seats. On the pole there's a rota for emptying them and we bury the stuff on the edge of the camp."

Two or three of the huts which faced the square had open fronts and outside them their owners sat crosslegged in the dust. One had fruit, in no better condition than the stuff Dig had picked up, while another offered a few buns and a couple of loaves of bread laid out on a cloth.

Chip licked his lips. "Are those shops?"

"Yes," Dig said, "but you can forget it. They're very expensive and only used by people too sick to get out and forage for themselves."

Sky was quite surprised to see how well organised the camp was. "The thing I don't understand about this place is, why do the Catchers let it stay here? I mean, why don't they come in, round everybody up and close the place down?"

44

"There's too many of us. They'd need an army to catch us all and those who escaped would only go and squat somewhere else, more visible. While we stay here they know where we are and we're out of sight, which is what the authorities want. Nowadays they like to play down the problem of street kids, particularly at a time like this when there's an election on. The Catchers may be called the 'Child Protection Unit', but you've got to understand, they exist to protect the adults from the children, not the other way round."

"What *really* happens to the people they catch?" Chip asked.

Dig sighed. "They're supposed to take us to the Care Camps."

"Have you ever seen one?"

"Yes," Dig admitted. "I did get picked up once by the Catchers."

"What was it like?" Chip asked.

"The camp? Oh, not so bad," Dig admitted. "They're just work camps really and at least it's a place to live and they feed you."

"That doesn't sound so awful."

"No," Dig admitted. "But you've got to work very hard in all kinds of weather and you lose all your freedom. You're stuck behind barbed wire and there's nothing to do apart from work. Mind you, in some ways the ones who end up in camps are the lucky ones."

"How do you mean?" Sky asked.

"Some kids caught by Catchers never get as far as the camps. Quite a few get shot. The Catchers swear they found the kids committing some crime or other, or that they tried to escape. But a lot of the kids they pick up are sold off."

"Sold, who to?"

"All kinds of people. Some get locked up in sweat

45

shops, illegal factories, others get sold to drugs barons as Mules, carrying drugs to the pushers. The Pushers are the ones to steer clear of. There are some here on the Tip. Half of them are on drugs themselves. They're always short of cash for their habits so they make perfect targets for Catchers who turn them into paid informers." Dig broke off and glanced up at the sun. "Come on, times are wasting, we'd better get to work."

As they were leaving the square, a large girl of sixteen or seventeen, her brown hair straying out of a large, untidy bun, walked towards the tap. She was dressed in a voluminous brown sack of a dress which reached down to her ankles revealing only her bare feet. In one hand she carried a large plastic bucket. Her other hand was clutched by a tiny child, whose other hand was, in turn, gripped tightly by the fist of a toddler. It was like a train, an engine towing two trucks.

"Berry," Dig called across, "come and meet Sky."

Berry kept pace with the little children as she walked slowly across. Both toddlers stared wide-eyed at Sky and Chip, while the one with a free hand sucked its thumb.

"Welcome," Berry smiled and when she did, Sky noticed, the whole of her peaceful, round face lit up. "Buzz told me you'd arrived. These two little ones are July and Popcorn. Go on, say hello." Neither child spoke, one kept its mouth firmly corked with its thumb. "I'm sorry, they're a bit shy of strangers. They'll be all right once they get to know you."

Sky asked awkwardly, "Are they yours?"

Berry laughed. "No, I've only been allowed to borrow them for the day. Mummy's busy, isn't she?" Then she added, quietly, "They're Feather's children, one of the older girls on the Tip. Every now and then she gets a washing-up job and she leaves them with

46

me in case they get scooped up for adoption by the Catchers."

"I didn't realise the Catchers adopted children," Sky said innocently and was surprised when both Berry and Dig laughed at her.

"Not exactly!" Dig exclaimed. "They collect kids to sell them for adoption."

"Sell?"

"I'm afraid so," Berry said. "Quite a few foreigners, who can't have children of their own and aren't able to adopt them in their own country, come here to buy one. The Catchers mostly round up the youngest kids they can lay hands on. Although babies fetch the highest prices they'll make do with kids like Popcorn or July if they're stuck."

Dig picked up the story. "Then, when the new parents turn up to collect, the Catchers pick up some girl off the street and pay her to pretend to be the baby's mother. Cherry and Babe often do it."

"Why do they need anyone to be the mother?"

"Somebody's got to forge a signature on the adoption papers and make it all look legal for the immigration people at the other end. Babe said the Catchers used to give her a raw onion to sniff before she went in to meet the new parents."

"What on earth for?"

"She was supposed to do a lot of crying and wailing and look as if she was going to change her mind at the last minute, swearing she couldn't bear to part with her child. That bumps up the price even higher, because these people have spent a lot of money travelling here and they don't want to go back empty handed."

Sky was indignant. "But if it's illegal, why don't the police stop it?"

"The same as with everything else," Dig said with

a shrug, "it gets more of us off the street and anyway, sometimes some kid gets a really nice home out of it."

Sky could hardly believe what Dig was saying but Berry nodded at every word.

"Berry, there's a lot Sky needs to know. Maybe some time later she could come and talk to you?"

"Of course."

"Just to get the feel of things," Dig said. "Their parents have just dumped them."

Sky resented being described like junk mail, but Berry was all sympathy. "You poor things! Come round this evening when I've put these little monsters to bed and then we can talk properly."

Seven

"I'll never be able to find a teddy bear in all that!" Chip said in disgust as he shaded his eyes against the sun and gazed up at the huge mountain of rubbish.

In the heat of the morning sun Sky found the stench, which had been bad enough during the cool of the evening, totally overpowering. Even the slightest breeze sent clouds of fine dust spiralling everywhere.

Sky, already convinced she could not only feel a thin coating all over her body, but could actually taste the stuff, snapped, "What did you expect, stupid? Everything in neat tidy piles? Tin cans over here, teddy bears over there! This isn't a department store, it's a rubbish dump."

Chip sighed. "Better make a start, I suppose."

Although Sky had to smile at his optimism, she felt she ought to prepare him for disappointment. "Look, Chip, there's so much junk up there, you might never find a teddy bear."

Chip nodded. "Then the sooner I get started . . ." and he began to climb the rubbish.

Dig hauled him back. "Be very careful. The Tip can be a dangerous place." Then he added gloomily, "I wish we weren't so late getting here. All the best spots, up at the top, have been taken."

Sky, for whom delving about in the litter bin outside the restaurant had been bad enough and who was dreading going on the Tip at all, was relieved that at least she wouldn't be expected to clamber through too much of the smelly stuff. "I don't see what difference it makes whether you're at the top or the bottom. It's all rubbish, isn't it?"

"Most of the new stuff's up there," Dig said, looking like a kid who's been shut out of a party, "but it's more dangerous too because you have to watch what the digger driver's doing. Some good stuff falls all the way down, but most of it's been thoroughly picked over by the people above, so the best's usually gone by the time it works its way down here."

"What exactly are we looking for?" Sky asked.

"Food's the most important. Like this chicken leg." He held it up for Sky to admire.

Sky felt sick. "It's covered in ashes!"

"They'll soon wash off." He casually brushed off some of the ash on the leg of his jeans and sniffed carefully at the meat. "At least it hasn't gone bad." He dropped the food into one of the big plastic carrier bags he had slung over his shoulder. "I keep one for food, one for useful things like tools or candle ends, that kind of thing, and the other's for stuff we can sell."

"What do you expect to sell from here?" Sky asked scornfully.

Dig shrugged. "All kinds of things. Scrap metal's best, but I've even sold broken toys and kids' push-chairs I've found on here. They all make money. Maybe it's only pennies but they buy bread."

Sky shook her head. "But if you can sell them, why does anybody throw them away?"

Dig grinned. "Most of it's chucked out by rich people who'd sooner have something new than get things mended. But there are plenty of poor people around who can't afford new and that's where we come in. It's all a question of knowing your markets

50

and contacts," he said knowledgeably. "You build those up after a while. That way you only try to sell the right things to the right people. Like this." He held up a screw-topped glass bottle. "It's one of the few you can still get back a deposit on, but I happen to know the only guy who'll give you the full amount. Most shops won't pay up because they know you didn't buy it in the first place."

Reluctantly, Sky bent down and was about to start turning stuff over when Dig stopped her.

"Not with your hands! There's jagged metal, broken glass and all sorts of things under there. I once came across a whole plastic bag of used hypodermic needles."

While he talked Dig turned things over with an old walking stick, picking out odds and ends which he sorted into the appropriate bags. Some of the Pickers had large baskets strapped to their backs.

"Believe me," Dig went on, "out here more people die from infected wounds than ever die of hunger. Better find yourself a stick like mine to search with. Oh, and never pick up anything you're not sure about. One day a kid picking next to me screamed like Hell. He'd tipped up a jar of acid. There was only a drop left in the bottom, but enough to burn all the flesh off his hand before we could do anything."

Chip, who'd been so anxious to get started, stood stiffly beside Sky, hardly daring to move.

Dig shook his head. "I tell you, nobody thinks about Throwaways, or cares what happens to us."

Sky found herself an old chair leg which was ideal for the job and began to scratch around in the debris. "The first thing I'd like to find is a peg for my nose. This smell is horrible!"

"You soon get used to it," Dig said. "I noticed it when I first arrived, but not any more."

Sky slowly began to turn over waste paper, broken

51

bottles and ash in the faint hope of finding something useful.

Dig called over again. "Keep an eye open for something sharp you could use as a knife. You need knives for all kinds of jobs and they're hard to come by. Buzz has got half a pair of scissors he's sharpened up. This is what I use."

He produced a circular top of tin, cut from a can. Half its vicious edge had been thickly bound with sticky tape to form a handle. "The jagged edge is very good for cutting through cloth, or rope. Oh, and another thing, I need some wheels, any kind of wheels. I want to build myself some sort of a cart to haul stuff into town more easily."

Sky prodded around with her chair leg, but her heart wasn't in searching through rubbish until she spotted some kind of furry toy, half hidden by a cereal packet. Thinking it might keep Chip happy, even if it wasn't a teddy bear, she called to him. "Hey, Chip, look what I've found!" But just as she was about to pick the toy up it turned and ran off!

Sky screamed.

Dig came running over. "What's up?"

"A rat. I nearly picked up a rat!"

"Oh, sure. The place is crawling with them, that's why I keep my food cabinet halfway up the wall, otherwise there'd be even less in it than there is now!"

After that, for about half an hour, Sky poked around more carefully but without success. Having been brought up not to pick up things in the street, Sky found it very difficult to re-programme her mind to accept the idea of plunging her hands into other people's refuse.

Yet all around her kids behaved as if it was the most normal thing in the world to have to fight off marauding crows and skinny mongrels for scraps of decaying food.

Chip had already lost interest. He'd tried to make friends with a mangy brown and black mongrel who'd come sniffing round his feet, but when he stretched out a hand to stroke it, the dog had snarled, baring its yellowing teeth.

"You want to leave the dogs alone," Dig warned. "They are riddled with disease, and some are mad with rabies."

Chip wandered off to sit on a rock some distance from the edge of the Tip and began playing with his toy truck.

Gazing round the other Pickers, Sky noticed a frail girl working just above them. To protect her from the sun's glare, she wore a battered straw hat and from beneath it trailed long wisps of hair, so blonde as to be almost white. She had tiny hands and the palest blue eyes Sky had ever seen. She caught Sky's eye and smiled.

"Hi, I'm Sky."

The girl nodded. "I know. Buzz put the word round. I'm Childie."

The name seemed especially apt. Because she was so small, Sky had thought Childie might be about Chip's age, but as soon as she spoke Sky realised that the girl was much nearer her own age. "We're only staying while we get ourselves sorted out," Sky said confidently, but she didn't enjoy Childie's knowing smile. "How long have you been living here?"

"Most of my life," Childie said with a smile.

Sky couldn't hide her surprise. "You were brought up here?"

Childie nodded. "I can't remember my parents, or what the family name is and, to be honest, I don't really know how old I am either."

Before Sky could say anything she was interrupted

53

by distant screams and a single voice shouting from higher up the Tip. "Look out below!"

As a few cans clattered past Sky glanced up. An avalanche of trash was sliding towards her in a cloud of dust.

Above it, at the very top, Sky could see a man in yellow overalls, presumably the lorry driver who'd just tipped his load over the edge. He was standing, hands on hips, watching the children as they tried to scurry to safety and escape the terrible danger he'd just unleashed on them. Sky was convinced he was laughing at them!

Dig shouted at Sky, "Don't *stand* there, clear off, out of the way!"

The truckload of rubbish gathered in size and speed as it fell, like a trail of lava running down from a volcano which collects up everything in its path.

By the time it had roared halfway down the slope, the swiftly moving pile had doubled in size. People and dogs were still rushing to get out of the way while irate seagulls squealed above them.

But Sky still hadn't moved. She was standing, mesmerised, directly in the path of the advancing wall, watching.

"Sky! Move! Now!" Dig ran back, grabbed her hand and tried to tug her to safety.

But even when Sky tried to move she quickly discovered that running across the shifting surface was not as easy as Dig had made it look. It was like trying to run across a pile of gravel.

In all the confusion and shouting, Sky suddenly heard a voice calling for help. She turned and saw that Childie was stuck immediately beneath the huge mass of tumbling rubbish. Having got her leg trapped in one of the treacherous hollows, she had fallen forwards and was struggling violently to free herself, but without success.

54

"Childie!" Sky screamed, as she and Dig ran back towards her.

But it was too late. The mound was moving too quickly for them. It charged on and Childie's pale, terror-stricken face disappeared, buried alive beneath the pile of rubbish as it swept by and crashed into the sea below.

"Watch your eyes," Dig warned, covering his own with his hands.

The violent movement over the surface of the Tip had thrown up a terrific dust cloud which rushed down the slope and enveloped them. Even though she had taken Dig's advice, Sky was left coughing and choking in the foul-tasting dust.

Long before the dust had settled, Dig was already running towards the spot where they had last seen Childie. "One down over here!" he shouted up the slope. "Childie's under this lot."

Ignoring all his own earlier words of caution, he feverishly began to dig with his bare hands. Like a dog using its front paws, he threw out a stream of cans, bottles, cardboard boxes and other scrap, in a desperate attempt to reach her.

The other Pickers all scrambled over to help, starting new, but smaller, slips of dust and rubble as they slid down the steep slope of the Tip.

"We'll never find her under all this," one boy said with tears in his eyes, but he kept on digging.

"Maybe she got swept away and was buried further down," another suggested.

Sky thought it must be impossible to pinpoint exactly where Childie lay under all the shifting garbage.

Dig was obviously having doubts too. Without looking up from his own digging, he complained, "We're all working on top of each other, spread out more."

Twenty or thirty children had been digging for ten minutes when Dig held up his hand. "Quiet!" he shouted. "Stay still a minute. I'm sure I heard something."

For a few seconds, except for the mournful cry of the disturbed seagulls wheeling overhead and the crash of the surf on the rocks below, the Tip was silent.

"We're wasting time," somebody complained.

But Dig irritably waved his hand until they all heard the voice which seemed to be coming from beneath their feet. "There she is!" Dig shouted. "Hold on, Childie, we're almost with you." Then he warned the Pickers, "Careful, we're getting close now and we don't want to hurt her any more than she is already."

More swift, but wary, digging revealed a tiny hand, clenching and unclenching. Next came a few wisps of Childie's white hair, her hat and finally, her pale face, streaked with ash.

"I think I'm all right really, it's just that I can't move," she said between coughs and splutters as they completed the job of unearthing her trapped body. It was freeing her hair that caused most problems. The long, fine strands had managed to get entangled in all kinds of objects so that, long after her legs and arms were free, several people had to struggle to unknot her.

"Nothing broken?" Dig asked.

"No," Childie said and then began to sob. "I'm sorry," she apologised. "I'm just a bit frightened, that's all. Has anybody seen my hat?"

Sky handed over the battered straw hat.

Four of the bigger boys, two on either side, joined hands and cradled Childie off the Tip and back to her hut.

Slowly the Pickers began to wander off, resuming

56

their work, though they were all badly shaken by what had happened.

"Having long hair isn't a good idea around here," Dig commented. "Apart from making it easier to get trapped, like Childie, it gives the Catchers more to grab hold of and you're more likely to get head lice."

Covered, as she was, from head to foot in grime and filth, Sky shuddered. "I'll ask Berry to cut it for me tonight." She was about to follow Dig when she glanced round and panicked. "Where's Chip? He didn't get buried too, did he?"

"No," Dig said firmly. "I'm sure he wasn't on the Tip."

"Then where is he? Last time I looked, he was sitting on that big rock on the edge of the Tip."

The boy who'd been crying during their search for Childie heard them talking and called over, "Are you looking for your brother?"

"Yes, have you seen him?"

"He was talking to Dozer earlier, I think they must have left together while we were busy rescuing Childie."

"Come on," Dig said grimly, "we'd better get after them."

He set off across the rubbish, leaving Sky to follow as best she could.

"Wait for me!" she called out to Dig. "What's the rush?"

"Do you want to see your brother again, or not?"

Eight

Dig kept up his breakneck pace as he led Sky through the maze of huts.

Breathlessly, as she struggled to keep up, Sky kept asking, "What's happened? Who's Dozer? Why are you so worried?"

Dig's answer left her none the wiser. "Dozer's a Keeper and his Ferret's sick."

"I still don't understand. What have ferrets or their keepers got to do with Chip?"

"Most of the people who live near the Tip are Pickers like me and we mostly stick together," Dig explained as he jogged between the huts. "Then there are the Mules, who run drugs, and some who thieve for a living, but the lowest form of animal life is the Keepers, like Dozer."

"But what *are* Keepers?" Sky asked as she stumbled along beside him.

"They live by thieving too; only they never do their own dirty work. Dozer keeps a Ferret, a kid called Tiny, to do the job for him. He bungs Tiny through gaps smaller than he could ever get through himself and then waits for Tiny to pass out the loot. He won't let Tiny climb out until he's brought him what Dozer reckons is enough."

Sky gasped, "That's terrible."

"That isn't the worst part," Dig said. "For a start it's the Ferrets, not the Keepers, who usually get caught. But the Ferrets are very valuable to the

Keepers. Think about it, without them they'd be out of business!"

"But how do they find people to do things like that?"

"They're often stray kids the Keepers pick up wandering round the city, who don't know any better. Sometimes they kidnap them. Either way, the Keepers promise to look after them and they certainly do! Once a Keeper's got hold of them, they never let the Ferrets out of their sight again. Dozer keeps Tiny chained up night and day. Even when they go out on a job, Dozer always takes him on a lead, like a dog, in case Tiny tries to do a runner. Worst of all, although none of us gets much to eat, the Ferrets are deliberately starved because that stops them growing too fat for their job."

"How awful!"

"About a week ago, Tiny cut his leg climbing out through a broken window and so Dozer's been on the lookout for a new Ferret. If we don't stop wasting our breath, the Ferret could be Chip."

"Oh, no!"

Dig halted abruptly outside an ominous-looking hut and banged loudly on the door.

It was built from over a hundred tea chests which had been stacked on their sides, ends out, to form the walls which had been roofed over with corrugated iron. Perhaps because of the strength and thickness of the chests, there was something about it, especially when compared to the flimsy huts either side, that gave an impression less of a shelter than of a fortress. A feeling which was emphasised by the door. It was the only metal one Sky had so far seen, having been taken off a huge refrigerator.

When nobody answered Dig's knocking he banged again, even harder. "Dozer, are you in there?"

Heads popped out of nearby huts, but nobody spoke and the metal door remained firmly closed.

Dig thumped the door once more before he wrenched it open and peered inside. The hut, having no windows, was in total darkness. Standing beside Dig, Sky could see nothing, though she was only too aware of a nauseating smell wafting through the open doorway.

"Tiny!" called Dig into the darkness. "Tiny, are you in there?"

A shaky, high-pitched voice came out of the gloom. "Yes, Dig, over here."

"Have you got a light?"

Sky heard several feeble attempts to strike a match before a pale, yellow glow established itself. Dig squatted in the open doorway. As Sky bent down and looked over his shoulder she saw a horrifying sight.

A small boy of about Chip's age was sprawled on a pile of dirty rags. He was so painfully thin that it was almost possible to count every bone in his body. This absence of flesh exaggerated the size of his eyes, which stared back at Sky like black saucers, and made the boy's skull seem too large for his emaciated body.

One of his stick-thin legs had a long gash down the thigh. Though partially covered by a grubby, loose bandage encrusted with congealed blood, the wound was still clearly visible. It oozed pus and was smothered in flies.

But what shocked Sky most, was the way he was tethered like an animal. Chains, which ran from his neck and one leg, were padlocked to a thick post driven into the earth floor.

Dig had other things on his mind. "Tiny, where's Dozer?"

"He was here a few minutes ago," Tiny said.

"Did he have a boy with him, about your age?" Dig persisted. Tiny nodded weakly. "Do you know where they went?"

"Dozer said something about them going into the city."

"Thanks, Tiny," Dig said. He was about to close the door when he casually asked, "How are you doing?"

"Not so bad."

"Need water or anything?"

The boy shook his head. The tea chests made the inside walls cellular, like a magnified bee's nest, and he pointed to one of the many openings where a half-empty bottle of water stood. "I wouldn't mind something to eat though," he said, hopefully. "Dozer hasn't brought me anything since yesterday."

Dig delved into one of his carrier bags and produced the chicken leg which he tossed over to Tiny. "Got to go, kid. See you later, maybe."

Tiny said through a mouthful of chicken, "Never give up, Dig."

"You too, Tiny," Dig said.

Dig had closed the door and was starting to walk away when Sky stopped him. "You're not leaving him there like that, are you?"

"Why not?"

"He's terribly ill. Didn't you notice that gash on his leg? He should at least see a doctor and he probably ought to be in hospital."

Dig looked pityingly at Sky. "Going anywhere near a doctor, or a hospital, is another way of handing yourself over to the Catchers. You'd hardly be in through the door before they were sent for. Get real!"

"So what happens when anyone's ill?"

"Either they cure themselves, or they catch the travelling surgery the nuns bring round each week. Look," Dig said angrily, "can we talk about this later? Tiny isn't going anywhere, but Chip is, and we've got to get to him before it's too late."

* * *

61

They'd passed the watchmen's hut and were crossing the railway tracks when they spotted Chip. He was on the other side of the sidings and he was with a big lad with greasy, black hair who was dressed in dirty jeans.

"There they are!" Dig said.

Sky shouted, "Chip!" as loud as she could, but a hoot from one of the engines drowned her out.

Bounding over the rails, they ignored the warning shouts of one of the drivers and narrowly avoided being crushed by some advancing trucks he was loose-shunting.

But by the time they'd reached the yard gate, Sky could see no sign of her brother, or Dozer.

"Now what do we do?" Sky demanded.

"Take a chance," Dig said, turning right out of the gateway and starting to jog down the street.

"And if you're wrong?"

"Too bad, but at least we'll have tried, instead of just arguing about it!"

"Why don't we split up? I could go the other way."

"Yes," Dig said grimly, "and the way your luck's running, you'd probably find them too! But I don't much fancy your chances against Dozer! No, come on, if we don't find them soon we'll turn back and try the other way."

But they didn't need to turn back. Moments later they saw the two, chatting happily together, as they strolled down a dim, side street flanked either side by tall warehouses.

Not until Sky called, "Chip!" did they even turn round.

But Dozer's fat, red face changed a great deal when he noticed Sky had Dig with her. He stood defiantly, feet apart, hands on hips. "Clear off, Dig. This is none of your business."

"But I'm going to make it my business, Dozer!" said

Dig, who was not only a head shorter than Dozer, but also only a third of his weight.

"Come here, Chip," Sky said crossly.

Chip looked baffled by all the fuss. "What's the matter? I'm only going with Dozer because, when I told him about losing Ted, he said he knew where I could get a brand-new one."

"Do as you're told!" Sky said. "Come here. Now!"

Chip was reluctantly about to obey his sister until Dozer caught hold of his arm. "Hang on! Surely you're old enough to make your own mind up, aren't you?"

"Yes," Chip agreed uncertainly.

"I mean," Dozer said with a curl of his lip, "you're not going to let a girl tell you what to do, are you?"

Chip shook his head, but he avoided looking at Sky.

"Dozer," Dig said, "give the kid back."

"Oh, yes? Or what?"

"I'll come and get him."

Dozer pushed Chip roughly behind him, into a doorway. "I'd like to see you try!"

"Okay." Dig quietly handed Sky the carrier bags he was still carrying.

Sky was getting worried. She could see that soon somebody was going to get hurt and, after Chip, the most likely person was Dig. "Don't, Dig! You can't fight him, he's too big."

But Dig wasn't listening. Never taking his eyes off Dozer, Dig walked slowly towards him. Dozer eased back, forcing Chip tightly into a corner of the doorway with his massive back, a mocking smile spread over his face.

Dig whipped out his can-lid knife and held it up, glinting in a shaft of sunlight, for Dozer to see. "Fancy getting cut, do you, Dozer?"

Dozer's smile faded slightly. "Hey, now, come on!"

"I *will* do it! Make no mistake, Dozer. I'll do it, if I

63

have to!" To make certain Dozer believed him, Dig took a sharp pace forwards.

Dozer tried to back away, but with Chip and the wall immediately behind him, there was nowhere for him to go. "Let's be serious!" Dozer said.

"Let the kid out!" Dig snapped.

For a second Dozer looked so angry that Sky thought he might throw himself on Dig, until Dig slashed the air with his knife only centimetres from Dozer.

To protect his sweating face, Dozer instinctively raised his forearm. "Hey, look," Dozer said, uncertain now. He pulled out Chip, who was crying, from behind him. "Take the kid if he means that much to you. He's too big for me anyhow!"

Chip ran to Sky. "How many times have I told you not to talk to strangers?" she asked, but she cuddled him against her legs.

Dig still threatened Dozer with his knife. "And stay away from him, got it?"

"Pardon me for breathing!" Dozer murmured as he thrust his podgy hands in his pockets and began to slouch away. Only when he'd gone a safe distance did Dozer pause and turn to call back to Dig, "You want to watch your back, Dig, mixing it with me! One dark night, you'll see, I'll have you!"

Nine

"I just don't feel I can live in a place like this," Sky declared.

It was evening and Sky, having left Chip sorting scrap under Dig's care with strict instructions not to let Chip out of his sight, was having her shoulder-length hair cut off by Berry.

She was sitting on an upturned box outside Berry's home, gazing over the rooftops towards the still, pewter-coloured sea. A line of gulls, having exhausted the pickings of the Tip, flew lazily down the jagged coast in a straggly line, black shapes against the skyline. The sun was setting, bronze beneath a strip of darkening purple cloud which promised the first rain for weeks.

Sky, feeling like a sheep which was being shorn, looked down glumly at the tufts of hair which lay in the dust around her feet. "The Tip is no place for me, let alone somebody of Chip's age."

Berry, who was snipping away, smiled gently. "I couldn't agree more."

"It's been a horrible day!" Sky said miserably. "Just think what could have happened to Childie. Or Chip, if we hadn't found him in time. He might have ended up like poor Tiny. And that's another thing! I went on and on at Dig, but he refuses to do anything to help Tiny."

Berry sighed. "Sky, there isn't much he can do. The Keepers think of the Ferrets as their property. They

65

all stick together and don't hesitate to use violence. You don't realise that, just by rescuing Chip, Dig's already taken an awful risk. He could be in tremendous danger. At least Chip didn't belong to Dozer, but on top of that if Dig helped Tiny to escape . . ."

Sky interrupted her. "But Tiny's leg desperately needs medical treatment and if he doesn't get some soon he could lose it altogether."

"I know all that," Berry nodded patiently. "But the only way to get him treated would be to get him out of here to the Free Hospital and even if Dig succeeded, all the Keepers would gang up into one army and hunt him down like an animal. Don't you understand? If they let Dig get away with taking Tiny from Dozer, anyone else could try to do the same. If that happened, all the Keepers would be put out of business."

"Good thing too!" Sky said emphatically.

"It happens I agree with you, but that isn't how things work. Life on the Tip is just the same as outside and the most important part has to be not what other people do, but your own survival. In your case that's doubly crucial because you've got the responsibility of looking after Chip."

"And a great job I've made of that!"

"You'll learn."

"I don't want to learn, not here. If I stayed on the Tip I don't suppose it would be long before I'd be forced to earn a living like Cherry. Either that, or I'll turn into a Keeper and start living off what Chip can steal."

"Not you," Berry said with a smile. "Besides, apart from that and Picking, there's plenty of other ways of earning a living."

"Such as?"

"Well, you only need a bucket and sponge to set yourself up in business washing windscreens when cars stop at the traffic lights. Mind you, that isn't very successful these days. Motorists, particularly women, tend to keep their windows wound up and drive off without paying since some kids have been reaching in to snatch handbags, or rip off jewellery. But Buzz makes a perfectly honest living selling newspapers by the railway station and Boots has a shoeshine stand."

"Yes, but we'd still be living here," Sky protested.

"Oh, it's not so bad when you get used to it, but there are alternatives."

"What, like giving ourselves up?"

Sky suddenly remembered Spindor, the Catcher who'd spotted her hiding in the basement. Was that really only yesterday? She couldn't help wondering, what would have happened to her by now if she'd been caught?

Berry answered Sky's thoughts by shaking her head so vigorously that another skein of hair escaped from the disintegrating bun. "No, I wouldn't recommend giving yourself up," Berry said. "There aren't many honest Catchers, so Lord knows where you might end up. No, I was thinking, you could get a place in one of the orphanages. It isn't that easy though, the nuns and monks who run them turn crowds of kids away every day. The other big problem is, they wouldn't allow you and Chip to stick together. Each one takes boys or girls, not both."

"Aren't you overlooking something? We're not orphans," Sky said firmly.

"As good as."

"Our parents aren't dead," Sky said stubbornly.

"Sky, they might just as well be for all the good they're going to do you now." Berry chose her words carefully and though they were harsh, her tone was gentle and she laid a comforting hand on Sky's shoulder. "The authorities won't waste money trying

67

to track them down, it's cheaper to put you in a Care Camp. No, they've gone for good, dumped you."

Sky shrugged away Berry's hand and snapped back, "You don't *know* that!"

But Berry pressed the point. "Most of us, particularly when we first arrive here, have dreams about our parents coming to take us away from all this and I grant you, it does occasionally happen. But not to most of us." Berry paused to wave her hand round the rickety shelters. "The truth is, *this* is your life from now on and it's only when you can face up to that and deal with it, that you can begin to make things better for yourselves. You've made a start here and got some friends, Dig knows his way around. Why not give it a go?"

Sky thought this was a curious situation in which to find herself. Having kicked against authority all her life and constantly complained about her parents always taking decisions without consulting her, now here she was, totally free to choose, except with so many down sides to everything. Sky simply resigned herself to the obvious. "I suppose I don't really have much choice, do I?"

"Not really. Not at the moment anyway. Your hair's finished. Want to see?" Berry held up a broken piece of mirror, its silvering pocked with rustmarks. "What do you think?"

Sky hardly glanced at the urchin cut she'd been given, but on her way back she soon began to feel the effects when large and surprisingly cold raindrops began to fall.

"Do you know which of these is bronze or copper and which is iron and steel?" Chip asked, anxious to display his new-found knowledge the moment Sky entered Dig's hut.

The floor looked like a scrapyard and Sky, soaked

by the sudden downpour, was forced to pick her way carefully through some dangerous-looking pieces of scrap metal. "Apart from being different shapes, they all look much alike to me," Sky admitted.

Chip held up two pieces of metal. "The one in my left hand's copper and this other one's bronze."

Dig, sitting back on his heels, pleased with the success of his new student, nodded in agreement. "What metal objects should you always be on the look out for?"

"Coins?" Chip suggested with an impudent grin.

"Yes, those too!" Dig laughed. "But what else?"

"Oh," light suddenly dawned for Chip, "drinks cans."

Sky was surprised. "Why those?"

"The city have a bounty on them," Chip explained proudly.

"Why?" Sky asked.

Chip looked at Dig to provide the answer. "Because they're so sick of the litter. They pay good rates for the old cans and get their money back from recycling the aluminium. Only trouble is, if we take them in to the collection centres the Catchers pick us up, so we have to sell ours to a middle man who gives us half as much and gets a profit, for doing nothing, when he sells them for the full price to the city."

"Well," Sky said, "you two have been busy while I've been gone."

"Oh, yes, and so has Berry by the look of you!" Dig said.

"You look like a boy!" Chip laughed.

"Thanks a lot!"

"You look fine to me," Dig said and then asked, "What's Berry been telling you?"

Sky noticed that Chip was not only watching her intently but, half-hidden behind his back, had his fingers crossed. A trick he'd long used for making wishes come true.

"She thinks we ought to stay here, at least for a while, until something better comes up."

"*Wicked!*" Chip shouted and bounced about.

Sky listened to the rain drumming on the iron roof while she waited for him to calm down a little. "All we need now is somewhere to live."

At that precise second, a blob of water that had seeped through a crack in the roof, dropped straight down the back of her neck. "Preferably," she added, "somewhere that doesn't leak."

It rained for two solid days. Streams of water ran down the hillside. Some followed the pathways, but much flowed through the flimsy huts, turning their earth floors into quagmires.

The Tip became even more unpleasant, turning into a huge cauldron of disgusting soup which mashed and oozed the moment anyone set foot on it. Consequently the Pickers not only had no work, but also no food.

Sky thought she had grown used to being hungry, yet the hunger pains she suffered during the rains were worse than anything she'd ever experienced.

"There's nothing we can do," Dig said. "We can't use the Tip and if we go all the way into the city, we'll get so wet we'll never be able to get our clothes dry."

They survived mostly on water and a few crusts of mouldy bread Dig managed to swap for some of his carefully hoarded scrap metal. By the second day food was so scarce amongst the Pickers that gold bars wouldn't have been able to buy it.

Aside from hunger, boredom was the worst enemy. Deprived of their usual activities and with no grown-ups offering helpful suggestions on how to spend the time, their day passed aimlessly. Chip soon got fed up with playing with his car. Dig either lay for hours on his tummy, drawing patterns in the mud floor with a stick, or rolled over to gaze out through the open window and watch the rain pouring off the roof.

"When it's like this," Dig muttered, "you can easily see how some kids get mixed up in drugs and glue-sniffing! Another week like this and even I might start drinking meths!"

Sky had far too much time to worry about her future. One thing she knew for certain, there was no way now that she would ever be able to fulfil her long-held ambition to become a nurse. Until Dad lost his job Sky had been getting on very well at school and had every hope of passing the necessary exams, but that hope had come to an abrupt end the moment they'd left home. Since then she'd never been in one place long enough to set foot in a school and coming to the Tip was the final straw.

Up to now her life had been full of fixed points which divided up her days and years. Between getting up and going to bed there had always been meals, going to school and TV programmes to watch. There were celebrations set by the calendar – birthdays, Christmas and holidays. Each provided points on a chart by which her life had been steered as surely as a ship navigates by sun, buoys and lighthouses.

Suddenly the charts were wiped blank. Sky was faced with featureless tracts of wide-open sea and both moon and sun were obscured by thick, dark clouds. No longer was there a compass to give her any sense of direction and she felt she was wandering, without destination and only accidental, unplanned ports of call.

Trapped in the hut, conversation was their only safety valve.

"If you were picked up by the Catchers and taken to one of the camps," she said to Dig, "how did you escape?"

"It wasn't easy. They guard those places so heavily and they have roll calls about every five minutes. In the end I hitched a ride out on the garbage truck. In the back, hidden under the rubbish and it brought me all the way back here! But I nearly ended up being thrown down the Tip with the rest of the rubbish when they emptied it. The guy driving it never slowed up once until he got here and even then he'd reversed right up to the edge before I could climb off. You should have seen his face when he saw me climbing out from under all that stuff!"

But it wasn't easy to talk without touching on forbidden subjects. Sky's thoughts were so often on her own parents that she couldn't help asking about Dig's.

His reluctant answer stuck to the basic facts. "Dad cleared off when my mum got sick. I looked after her for quite a while, but when she died I'd nowhere else to go."

"How long ago was that?"

"About four years. I must have been Chip's age when one of the street mothers, Golden, she's gone now, picked me up like I did you two."

Sky wondered what it must be like to live on the Tip for four years, and hoped she would never find out.

During hurried trips to the lavatories, or the standpipe, jumping pools and skidding on the treacherous surface of the wet ground, Sky kept an eye open for a site where they might be able to build their own hut.

At first there seemed to be no room left. Then she began seriously looking at minute spaces between huts, some so small it would have been impossible for Chip to creep in on his own.

"There's nowhere," she said, shaking the water off herself like a dog after another despairing search.

"Wait until the rain stops," Dig kept saying. "We'll find somewhere.

The winds which accompanied the rain on the second day blew away several of the tents and some of the flimsier huts were washed away. Those made of cardboard, while they could survive showers, under the torrential rain, slowly disintegrated into brown porridge.

When the rain stopped, after a lengthy search, Sky and Chip did find a site. Although it was a long way from Dig's hut, on the edge of the shanty town, at least that also meant it was as far from the smell of the Tip as possible.

Sky was impatient to move in but Dig laughed. "You've got to build it first! That could take weeks," Dig had pointed out. "You've got to find all the materials, which won't be easy because you've still both got to eat every day. It'll be the same with building it too. After you've spent the day Picking and selling, that only leaves the evenings to work on the house."

Sky had been very dejected until she hit on the idea of getting everybody else to help. "I saw it in an old film once. Somebody's barn had been burned down, so they'd nowhere to store their harvest, and people came from miles around and helped, so they were able to put up this massive new barn in a single day."

"But that was only a story!" Dig said scornfully. "In real life, especially around here, people have enough problems looking after themselves without bothering about anyone else. Besides, you're still new. You've only been here just over a week. I'll help, so will

Berry and maybe one or two others, but mostly they don't take that quickly to newcomers."

Sky considered the problem and came up with a surprising solution. "We'll bribe them!"

"Oh yes? How?"

"The reason it'll take us so long is mainly because we spend most of our time looking for food, isn't it?"

"Yes."

"Well, that applies to everyone else too. So, what if we turn the whole thing into a party and promise food for everyone who helps?" Sky said triumphantly.

"I think it's a brilliant idea, Sky. The only problem is, if you have a struggle feeding yourself, how are you going to feed everybody else as well?"

"Buns and cakes," Chip said suddenly.

Dig and Sky stared at him.

"You know the baker's shop I sometimes call in at on the way back from the Tin Man's scrap yard? Doughy often gives me old bread and stuff."

"Get real!" Dig scoffed. "If it was that easy to persuade people to give us food, why don't we do it that way all the time? He may give you the odd stale bread roll to ease his conscience, but that isn't the same as asking him to hand over enough to feed an army. Outsiders don't like street kids, they wouldn't care if all the Throwaways starved to death."

But Chip had said, "There's no harm in asking."

When they next took a bundle of scrap to sell to the Tin Man, on the way back, Chip popped through the back door of the baker's and returned empty-handed, but bearing the amazing news that Doughy was willing to help.

"Are you certain?" Sky asked. Dig had poured so much cold water on her idea that she'd begun to believe her plan would never work.

"Yes," Chip said proudly. "I told him what it was for, to get people to help us build a hut. I promised I

74

wouldn't bother him again for a whole month and that he could just keep what he usually gives me each visit and I'd collect it all in one go. He wasn't keen at first, but in the end he said, just this once!"

"Brilliant!"

Ten

A couple of days after the rains had stopped, people were out at work again, Chip was picking on the Tip with Dig, when the camp got some unusual visitors.

Sky had just returned from a long and not very successful trip, scavenging in the city. Although she'd managed to find a stool, she'd brought back little food. She was putting three bruised oranges and half a loaf of bread, which she'd found in a bin near the Bus Station, into Dig's store cupboard, when she heard an urgent beat on the metal drum.

The Pickers were already scrambling down from the Tip as Sky joined a thin stream of people all hurrying from their huts towards the centre of the camp.

On their way, several armed themselves with sticks and other impromptu weapons, which they kept concealed, waiting to find out what was going on. When they arrived they formed a silent, uneasy semicircle.

Amongst the crowd Sky noticed Childie, looking frailer than ever beneath her ragged straw hat; Berry was also there, her two charges clinging to her skirts. Sky wondered if it was she who had thoughtfully hidden the illicit standpipe under a pile of firewood.

Packed into the still boggy square were several vehicles, including two Catchers' vans, a minibus and a 4-wheel drive jeep.

Men and women, some with cameras, were jumping

down from the minibus and the Catchers seemed to be providing a guard of honour for a fat man in a white suit who was very concerned about the mud which was spoiling his fancy white shoes.

Sky immediately recognised him as the well-fed, smug-looking man whose photograph appeared on the election posters she'd seen in the city. She also wondered if one of the four Catchers might turn out to be Spindor, but they were all strangers.

Nobody spoke during the preparations and some of the journalists stared coldly at the ragged collection of youngsters as if they were on exhibition.

But the children, far from being annoyed or intimidated, merely kept their distance and stared back.

Sky slowly became aware that their confidence didn't spring simply from the fact that they outnumbered the visitors, but more from the huge, collective wave of hostile energy she sensed the group was generating, all aimed directly at the Outsiders.

Some of the photographers were about to take a shot when a thin man deliberately stood in their way, his arms held wide. "Gentlemen, hold on a minute! Let's get things organised here; we'll provide a proper photo opportunity for you in a moment." He turned and almost bowed towards the fat man. "Mr Stin?"

Mr Stin, carefully picking his way past his Minder and through the puddles, placed himself between the photographers and the rapidly growing number of children as Pickers from the Tip continued to arrive.

"What's going on?" Chip asked, sidling up to Sky.

She shook her head. "I don't know."

Berry whispered, "They do this for every election. It's the only time any grown-up Outsider ever comes down here and, believe me, it isn't for our benefit. He's just using us."

With an oily smile, Mr Stin began to address the journalists. "Gentlemen, as you know, during the current election campaign, a number of my misguided opponents have been mouthing off a lot, about my policy in relation to the growing number of street children. So I've brought you here today to experience, for yourselves, the alternative to my Child Protection Units and the carefully organised programme of Care Camps which I set up to look after these unfortunate children."

For the benefit of the photographers, he turned with a dramatic sweep of his hand to display the semicircle behind him and for a split second Sky saw that, despite the apparent smile, his grey eyes were so cold as to be almost dead.

He held the pose until the flashlights were still again before he continued. "Sad to say, many of these deprived, undernourished children, sadly known as Throwaways, have been cruelly abandoned by their parents and left to live in the squalid conditions you see around you, scraping a living as best they can. Not surprisingly, many rapidly fall into a life of crime. Theft, drugs and prostitution become a way of life for them and every year hundreds of these innocent victims perish, some in horrendous circumstances. It was to rescue them from this terrible life of disease and degradation, that I created the Child Protection Unit, some of whose gallant officers you see here with us today."

More clicking and whirring of motor-driven cameras as the photographers focused on the Catchers.

"Gallant officers!" Dig spat the words out under his breath.

A woman journalist near the front of the group spoke up. "Mr Stin, what answer do you give to the allegations that the Catchers, as they're better known, have been selling children they capture into slavery and that they're also responsible for some of their deaths?"

Mr Stin held up his hand. "Amber, there'll be plenty of time for questions later. After we've briefly adjourned to the Hilton Hotel, for a small buffet I've laid on, I'd like you to contrast the conditions that exist here in this shameful shanty-town with those in my own Care Camps." Mr Stin paused momentarily. His voice trembled with emotion when he began again. "I know there are some who criticise my spending on the Child Protection programme, but I think you've only got to glance around you. Surely, if we can bring a little light and comfort into the lives of these poor, unhappy children, then it's money well spent?" Mr Stin, like a man ending a prayer, left another dramatic pause before he checked his watch and briskly added, "And now, if you've got all the photographs you need, we should be on our way. We're on a very tight schedule and your wine'll be getting warm!"

A few journalists laughed politely, but one of the photographers detached himself from the group and placed himself squarely in front of Mr Stin. "I'd like a couple of close-ups, Mr Stin."

"Sure, Jay!" Mr Stin smiled. "How would you like me?"

"With one of the children," Jay replied.

Mr Stin's smug look vanished. "You should realise, Jay, that these kids are laden with germs and disease. Head lice, ringworm and Lord knows what besides. I'd hate you to expose yourself to any risk of infection."

"Don't worry, Mr Stin." Jay smiled broadly. "I'm made of pretty strong stuff myself and if you don't mind, I'm sure it would make a great photograph for your campaign. You know, showing the 'caring' face?"

Trapped, Mr Stin growled at his Minder, "Boy, you heard what Jay said, and make sure it's a reasonably clean one!"

The Minder glanced quickly round the assembled children with an experienced eye which instantly lit on the innocent, pathetic face of Childie. "You, the one in the straw hat, you come here." But Childie shook her head and tried to huddle back into the group. "I said come here, we don't have all day. Officer!"

One of the Catchers roughly pushed his way through the children towards Childie saying, in a voice too low to be caught by the watching journalists, "Don't make it tough on the others, kid. We could always come back after this circus has moved on and pick a few of you up!"

With a sigh, Childie reluctantly followed the Catcher out to the front. Though she was sulking, even Mr Stin could see that Childie, with her pale skin, paler hair and huge, appealing, pale blue eyes peering out from under the tatty straw hat, was the perfect choice. "Look at this poor waif," Stin said, "and consider her likely fate if we don't rescue her from her wretched situation."

Mr Stin placed a seemingly protective arm around Childie's shoulder and used it to drag her closer to his fat little body.

Jay's camera clicked several times. "That's great, Mr Stin. Just one more."

But Mr Stin, beginning to wonder if the readers who saw this photograph might take more notice of the girl than of him, held up his hand. "That's enough now, Jay."

As the reporters trailed away Sky, to her amazement, heard Stin say in an undertone to his Minder, "Have one of the Catchers get this one scrubbed off, given clean clothes and bring her round to my place tonight."

"No!" Childie protested.

But it was too late. The Catcher who'd brought her out of the crowd held her firmly by the wrist.

Hearing the disturbance, the woman reporter, Amber, turned back. "What's going on?"

Mr Stin cut in quickly. "Nothing at all, Amber. It's just that we've tried to offer a place in one of my Care Camps to that little lady, but she, misguidedly, doesn't want to go." He sighed deeply. "I'm afraid some of these children are very prone to believe all the ugly rumours you people keep spreading in your newspapers. Which only serves to make the Protection Officers' job more difficult."

As the group wandered away, Sky could see that, although she was struggling to free herself, the Catcher still had a firm grip on Childie. Sky, convinced that the moment the Press were out of sight Childie would be bundled into the Catchers' van, broke the silence. She called out at the top of her voice, "If you want to see something really awful you should come down here!"

Everyone in the square, Pickers and journalists alike, turned.

"What was that you said?" Jay asked.

"Oh, I'm sure it was nothing," blustered Mr Stin.

"Shut up, Sky," Dig hissed, "before you get us all in big trouble!"

"I heard her," Amber piped up. "She said, something about 'if you want to see something really awful . . . '."

"All hot air, I'm sure," Mr Stin said, feeling events were getting out of his control. He dug his Minder viciously in the ribs. "Boy, we're way behind schedule already, get them all back in the bus."

In an attempt to propel her in the right direction, Mr Stin grabbed Amber's arm.

But Amber wasn't satisfied. Pulling herself free,

she walked back towards the children. "Who was that who shouted out just now?"

Sky raised her hand. "Me." She was very aware that the others around her, including Chip, were carefully separating themselves from her.

"And what was it you wanted us to see that was so awful?" Amber smiled encouragingly.

Sky swallowed and spoke out. "There's a boy, Tiny, chained up in that hut over there." She pointed towards Dozer's hut.

Amber smiled disbelievingly. "Oh, come now!"

"It's true!" Sky said, her mouth growing dry as the other children ignored her and stared at the ground. Though she could not see their eyes, she was aware that the hostile group energy, originally directed at the Outsiders, was now focused on her, but she continued regardless. "He's got a terrible wound on his leg, but he can't escape to get it treated and he's probably going to die if something isn't done soon."

In the silence which followed Sky noticed with relief that the Catcher had released Childie, who'd quickly melted away into the crowd.

"Ladies and gentlemen," Mr Stin, who was growing very agitated, called out, trying to gain their attention. "These children often make up stories, simply to draw attention to themselves. Pathetic, of course, but I'm sure you understand . . ."

But the photographer, Jay, who'd gained his impressive reputation through exploring far more outrageous leads to stories than this one, wasn't convinced. "Okay, Mr Stin, but if it's not too much trouble, I'd like to check it out for myself," he drawled. Jay swiftly weaved his way through the throng of people towards Sky. "You lead the way, kid," he said gently.

"I really think. . ." Mr Stin said loudly, but nobody was listening, they were all following Sky and Jay.

82

Mr Stin knew he'd lost the limelight and had no alternative but to go with them. "I blame you for this!" he snapped at his Minder.

Surrounded by journalists and photographers, the closer they came to Dozer's fortress, the more doubts grew in Sky's mind. Although she'd always wanted to find a way of helping Tiny, her original plan had been simply to divert attention from Childie, so that she could escape. She'd never thought for one moment that any of the visitors would either believe her, or want to do anything about Tiny. What would happen to her now if Dozer had spirited Tiny away? She also remembered Berry's warning and wondered what Dozer would do to her if they did find Tiny?

It was Jay who pulled open the refrigerator door and crawled inside the hut. Seconds later those out-side saw the interior lit vividly several times by his camera's electronic flash.

Jay crawled out, white-faced. "I've been through five civil wars all round the world and I've seen some dreadful things in my time, but nothing to beat that! There's a sick kid, shackled to a post in there! You'd better get an ambulance down here, right away!" he said to Mr Stin.

Angry reporters demanded to know, "How can you claim your so-called Protection Plan is the answer when things like this are going on?"

Mr Stin avoided answering by busying himself giving orders, telling one Catcher to call an ambu-lance and sending another to find some bolt-cutters.

Tiny was gently carried out, blinking in the un-accustomed sunlight, and whimpering with pain. In broad daylight his festering wound looked even worse than it had by candlelight. Also there were angry patches where the chains had chafed his skin and he had dark circles beneath his eyes.

As they waited for the free ambulance to arrive,

Sky happened to look up and saw Dozer, tucked well away in the crowd, gazing at her with intense hatred.

After Tiny, Jay, Amber and a very angry Mr Stin, still desperately trying to wipe the mud off his splattered white trousers, had all gone, the crowd of children quickly dispersed.

Sky was walking slowly back with Dig and Chip when Dozer appeared ahead of them from between two of the huts and blocked their path. "You really don't know when to keep your nose out, do you?" He spat the words at Sky. "Just you wait, one day I'll stitch you up good and proper!" Then he turned and strode off.

"In a way, he's right," Dig said.

"You think I was wrong to find a way of helping Tiny, don't you?"

"Yes, I do," he snapped.

Sky couldn't understand his thinking. "Why?"

"For a start, we *never* involve Outsiders."

"Not even when somebody's dying?"

Dig shook his head. "Not even then!"

"I think you've been living this way too long, Dig. All Outsiders aren't bad. Look at the baker who's giving all that food."

"Yes, well, I'll believe that when it happens too. But don't you see," Dig was sounding quite angry, "what you did today puts us all in danger? Other kids, long gone, struggled for years to get this place going, so it doesn't belong to any one person and none of us has the right to destroy it. What you did today gives the Catchers all the excuse they need to come back and clear this whole site. Where would we all be if they tried to burn us out?"

Sky was horrified. "Burn?"

"They often 'accidentally' set fire to a few of the huts and then it spreads like wildfire. With a

84

struggle, we usually manage to put them out, but one day . . ." Dig shook his head.

Sky stubbornly kicked a stone and watched it roll away. She'd come to respect Dig's views, admire him even, and the strength of the anger he was directing at her stung very deeply. Desperately, she tried to justify her actions. "Well, at least my way Tiny might not die."

"Oh, no," Dig said bitterly, "he probably won't, but now that you've interfered, what do you think he'll do when he comes out of hospital? If he isn't sent straight to one of the Care Camps, how's he going to earn a living? If he'd lost that leg he might have done better as a beggar because, let me tell you, he'll never be able to come back near the Tip, not while Dozer's still around. And I'll tell you something else, you're lucky they took photographs of Tiny, because if they hadn't that would have been the last you'd ever have seen of him, in this world anyway!"

Sky stood silent, trying to hide her injured feelings.

"Still," Dig suddenly sighed, "I don't suppose any of it matters. It's them descending on us like a pack of rats that makes me so mad, but you shouldn't play into their hands. It's not as if they'll change anything. We shan't set eyes on them again until the next election comes round and they've all gone off to enjoy a slap-up meal at Stin's expense, although you notice they didn't think to bring us so much as a crust of bread! You can bet by tonight we'll all be forgotten when they're all tucked up safely in their big, smart houses."

Eleven

In the end it took five weeks of scrimping and searching to collect what Dig thought would be enough materials to build a reasonable-sized hut. They wouldn't have taken quite so long, if some of the wood they'd found hadn't been stolen from behind Dig's hut where it was stored.

During that time, as Dig had predicted, they worked like dogs. Apart from finding planks, plastic sheeting and all the other building materials they needed, they'd also had to work and fight the never-ending battle against hunger.

While they still lived with him, Dig shared everything with them, but Sky was keenly aware that as soon as they had their own hut, that must end. By then they would have to be totally self-supporting.

In some ways she wasn't sorry. Although Dig had calmed down since their argument over Tiny, things had never been quite the same between them again and, sadly, she knew he would always regard her as part Outsider.

Sky felt she'd only strengthened his opinion when she suggested that they should go and visit Tiny in hospital.

"Oh, very smart!" he replied. "Take him a bag of half-rotten oranges and get scooped up by the Catchers before you can find out which ward he's in!"

Buzz hadn't helped matters by bringing back, a couple of days later, one of his unsold evening newspapers which prominently displayed, across three columns of the front page, two photographs of Tiny. The first was of Tiny still chained up in Dozer's hut, while the second showed him happily recovering in the Free Hospital.

"There you are!" Sky defiantly waved the paper at Dig. "The surgeon says: 'Tiny won't lose his leg, but it was touch and go, he only arrived in the nick of time'."

Dig grabbed the paper, looked at the photograph and tossed it aside.

"Take it easy!" Buzz complained. "That newspaper's got to be fit to go back tomorrow or they'll take it out of my wages."

They both ignored him.

"All down to me," Sky said proudly.

"Yes," Dig said bitterly, "and is it 'all down to you' that the other day six kids on their way back to the Tip were picked up by the Catchers near the night-watchman's hut? And I suppose you'd also like to claim responsibility for the Public Health people we've had snooping about the place?"

Sky further increased the gulf between herself and Dig by rarely going Picking. Dig didn't criticise her for this, but several times he half-jokingly suggested that it was because she thought herself "a cut above the Pickers".

Quite simply, she loathed the horrible smell, but there were other reasons too. After Childie there had been several similar slips, and the Tip really terrified Sky.

But finally what turned her against Picking was an experience during her last visit.

She'd been picking through a pile of dirty rags when suddenly a piece of metal caught her eye. She snatched it up immediately and although it was very battered and bent out of shape, and part of it had broken off completely, Sky was convinced it was the back of the hairbrush she'd been given for her ninth birthday. The one which had been carried away together with their car.

"Chip, come and look what I've found."

Chip took it from her and examined it, but quickly tossed it back. "That isn't silver if that's what you thought."

She had always believed that it was. "I wasn't asking for you to value it. Don't you know what that is?" Chip shook his head. "That's the backing off my hairbrush."

"So?"

"That was in the suitcase with all my other belongings."

"And?"

"Don't you understand? If this is here, all our other things must be here too."

"So what? None of my clothes would fit me and you've got so thin lately, I don't suppose yours would either."

"But they're *our* things, part of our past."

She'd been about to mention the family photograph, which had been in the same suitcase as the brush, together with the mouth organ, but was glad she hadn't when Chip dismissed the subject with a wave of his hand. "That was a million years ago."

She clambered off the Tip and walked down to the edge of the sea, still clutching the fragment of metal. "I suppose he's right," she said to herself. "It's no use trying to cling on to the past."

She threw the piece of metal as far out to sea as she could and watched it disappear. Once it was gone she wished she hadn't let it go, but it was too late and after that she never went Picking on the Tip again.

Chip, on the other hand, had become an excellent Picker, often spotting pieces of metal Dig passed over.

Dig joked that Chip had an unfair advantage. "It's easier for him to see things because he's closer to the ground!"

But Sky was startled, when she took the time to look properly at her brother. She hadn't realised how much he'd grown up in the short time they'd been living at the Tip. It was impossible to imagine him as the little boy who had, not so long ago, been constantly demanding either to be carried, or for Sky to tie up his laces. Though his brown velvet eyes were still fringed by his gloriously long lashes, his face was much older, like many of the other children on the Tip whose faces and bodies looked like those of miniature, middle-aged men.

Not only was he taller, he was tougher too. Both physically and mentally. He hardly ever mentioned their parents any more and his search for a replacement Ted had long been abandoned.

The fact that he had undoubtedly adapted to life on the Tip far better than Sky wasn't entirely a source of comfort to her. His rapid and complete acceptance of a way of life which, to her, was not only unpleasant, but where crime and violence constantly lurked in the background, bothered her.

When Chip returned like a working man, tired and filthy after a day's Picking, weighed down with scrap, she greeted him with mixed emotions. Although she was relieved that it meant they would be able to eat the following day, she couldn't forget that he was in reality a six-year-old who ought to be out playing with his friends and going to school to learn to read and write.

Eventually the day arrived when everything for building their hut was ready. Chip and Dig had bruised thumbs from spending every evening for a week straightening nails they'd pulled from broken boxes. Sky had added to their collection of the make shift furniture.

On his way back from the scrapyard Chip warned the baker he'd be back the following day at five to collect the food. Sky wrote a note on the back of an old envelope she'd found and using two bits of unlicked gummed flap, stuck it to the pole.

HUT BUILDING PARTY
Tomorrow night
Sky and Chip invite you to join them
(next to Famous Pinhead's)
to try to build a hut
in one evening.
Materials supplied, please bring tools.
! ! ! ! FREE CAKES & BUNS ! ! ! !

Sky was relieved when, during the evening, several people called round at Dig's hut to say they'd definitely be there to help. Though not so thrilled that Guts intended to be one of them!

That night the three of them were lying in the dark, listening to the dogs barking, ready to go to sleep, when Sky said, "Just think, Chip, tomorrow night we could be sleeping in our own home!"

"Good thing too!" Dig interrupted sleepily.

Sky, by using the phrase "our own home" had conjured up a whole series of memories of the home she'd shared with her parents. Unlike Chip, a day never passed for Sky without her wondering where they were and what they were doing. Lying under an old car rug, on a mattress made of sacks filled with screwed up newspaper, Sky couldn't help remembering her old room with the comfortable bed she'd had. Who was renting their old house now and would one of them be sleeping in her bed?

"You'll be glad to get rid of us, I suppose?" Sky murmured.

"Not so much you, as all the junk you've got littering up the place!"

Having had the wood stolen, Sky had insisted on storing the furniture she'd managed to find inside Dig's hut, making it unbearably crowded.

"Dig?" Sky said quietly.

"What?"

"Thanks for all your help," she said. "We'd never have managed without you."

Dig sounded as if he was almost asleep as he mumbled, "Forget it."

After a lengthy pause she said again, "Dig?"

"What now?"

"Everything's going so smoothly, you do think it'll be all right, don't you?"

"It won't if you don't let me go to sleep," he said crossly. "Good night!"

There had been another hut on their chosen site and they spent most of the following morning clearing away the remains, levelling it off and piling up any useless wood they found.

"We can have a bonfire tonight," Dig suggested. "It'll give us extra light to work by and help keep us warm."

Towards the end of the afternoon, Sky and Chip set off to collect the food from the baker's.

Because she had no control over it, this was the part of the plan which made her nervous. "I'll wait outside for you."

The street was busy with people all making their way home from work and she was content to sit on the wall opposite one end of the entry and watch them, while Chip went in through the back door of the bakery.

Suddenly, further up the street amongst the crowd, she caught sight of the back of a man's head. Although it was only a brief glimpse, there was something about the corn colour of his thinning hair and the jaunty angle of his head which convinced Sky that it was her father.

She wanted to call out, but was frightened he might run away and leave her again. Instead she began to run, weaving in and out of the people, trying to catch up with him.

A group of workmen, climbing down from a lorry, got in her way and by the time she'd fought her way through them, and their tool bags, Dad had gained considerably on her.

Pausing to jump up amongst the crowd, so as to get a better view, she saw him turning left, but when she reached the corner and burst out on to the main street, there was no sign of him.

The street swarmed with pedestrians and traffic. Sky narrowly avoided getting herself knocked over by a bus which pulled up and blocked her view.

Quickly, she ran clear of it, to see if he'd crossed the road, but still couldn't find him. Then as Sky turned back, disappointed, she realised that she'd run past him!

He was one of the people queuing to board the already overcrowded bus.

Sky frantically elbowed her way through the queue of protesting passengers until he was immediately ahead of her, reaching out for the handrail, his foot already on the step. In seconds he would be gone.

She lunged forwards, grabbed his arm and shouted, "Dad!"

But when he turned his head, Sky saw that he was a total stranger.

"I'm sorry," she stammered her apology. "I thought you were somebody else."

As the passengers roughly pushed her aside and the bus drove away, Sky was left to swallow her disappointment.

Slowly, she made her way back and when she reached the entry, saw that parked at the opposite end was a Catchers' van.

She was convinced that while she'd been away chasing her dream, the Catchers had picked up Chip. Without thinking of her own safety, Sky ran down the entry shouting his name over and over.

Any moment she expected to see the van pull away, but she reached it and thumped its side with her clenched fist.

Chip banged back and called out, his voice muffled and frightened. "Sky, get me out of here."

The Catcher, it was Spindor, leaned out of the open cab window, chewing gum. "Hi. You're the one I saw hiding in that basement, aren't you? This kid's yours, is he?"

"Yes, and I want him back."

"Now, hold on a minute!" Spindor said, climbing slowly out of the van. There was no sign of his partner. "It isn't as simple as that."

Sky ran up to Spindor and tugged at his uniform shirt. "He's my brother and I want him back."

Spindor released her grip and waved her away as if she was a troublesome fly. "Now, take it easy, no need to get agitated."

"Yes, there is, you've got Chip! He's the only family I've got left and I'm not going to be separated from him."

"Oh, that could be easily settled," Spindor said, "if I take you as well."

Sky fell silent and stepped back against the wall. "No!" she said.

"Oh! Now, you're not so bothered if I take your brother, as long as I leave you behind?"

"That's not what I meant!" Sky said, but flushed with guilt because she knew, when it came right down to it, that he was right.

But he showed no sign of doing anything. Instead Spindor perched his sunglasses on the top of his wavy, blond hair, folded his arms and leaned a broad shoulder against the side of the black van. He cocked his head on one side and examined Sky carefully. "How long have you been living on the streets?"

"A month or so."

"How come?"

"Our parents dumped us."

"And where do you live?"

Sky was catching the Tip habit of being suspicious of people who wanted to know too much. "You ask a lot of questions, don't you?"

Spindor gave a slow, easy smile. "I'm entitled." He jerked his thumb at the van. "Remember, I've got your brother locked up in here."

"I live on the Tip," she admitted.

"I see," he said thoughtfully. "You make a living as a Picker?"

"Yes, we do, if you can call that living."

Spindor eased himself on to the other shoulder, but his dark brown eyes never left her face. "Never been tempted into anything else? Drugs and stuff?"

"No."

"Your brother too? I mean he's not being used by a Keeper?"

"No. The only things we've taken are things nobody else wanted, things they've thrown away."

"Is that right? Thing is, I just found him with two carrier bags stuffed full of cake and buns."

"I can explain those . . ."

"I'd be interested to hear."

"The baker back there gave them to Chip."

"You realise I can easily check?"

94

"Yes. That's why it'd be stupid to lie, wouldn't it?"

This time Spindor laughed, deepening the lines around his mouth and eyes, which glowed with admiration. "I like your style, kid."

Sky wasn't sure she wanted the approval of a Catcher. "My name is Sky," she said firmly.

"Sky," he said rolling it around in his mouth, trying it on for size. "Suits those amazing eyes of yours."

Sky shifted uneasily. She remembered all Dig's warnings about the children the Catchers picked up, the ones who never arrived at the Care Camps, and she also remembered the way Mr Stin had slavered at the prospect of getting his fat paws on Childie.

"I wonder why Doughy gave you all that food?"

She explained about the hut-building party they'd arranged and then shrugged. "But I don't know why Doughy agreed to give us all the stuff." She was beginning to wonder if he'd only agreed in order to set a trap for them. Maybe it was Doughy who'd called the Catchers.

"Oh, I do!" Spindor nodded. "Doughy was once a Picker too! Most don't live long enough to make it off the Tip, but he did."

"So he didn't get you to come and pick us up?"

Spindor shook his head. "No, he didn't. Matter of fact, I'm here waiting for my partner. Shakey's got a lady-friend – lives over the road."

Although Sky began to feel a glimmer of hope, despite his easy smile she still didn't trust him. "What are you going to do about us?"

"Do? I'll show you." Spindor pulled from his trouser pocket a huge bunch of keys, attached to a shiny, chrome chain. He walked round to the back of the van and unlocked the door.

Inside one of the wire cages, six down either side, Chip, red-eyed, was crouched on the floor.

Sky, not knowing quite what Spindor intended,

hung back. But Spindor hopped in and unlocked Chip's cage. "Stand up, Chip."

Chip did as he was told. Badly frightened, he no longer looked older than his years, but was back to being just a tear-stained little boy.

Spindor jumped out of the van and lifted Chip down on to the road. "My partner should be nearly done by now. It would be embarrassing for me if you were still around when he returns."

Sky caught hold of Chip's hand. "We won't be, I promise! And thanks."

"Don't thank me, just don't let me see either of you again. Next time I may have no choice." Sky turned and was about to run off when Spindor called her back. "Aren't you forgetting something?" He held out two bulging carrier bags which he'd been keeping in the cab.

"Thanks."

"You're welcome. Hope the hut works out, but remember what I said. Don't let me see you again and don't forget, Doughy's an exception. Not too many kids survive the Tip."

"You were locked in the cage and he just turned you loose?" Dig had been amazed by the whole story of their encounter with Spindor.

Chip nodded. There was no sign of tears now that he was back safely and the more questions Dig asked, the more puffed up with pride, at having escaped, Chip became.

"I've never heard of a Catcher letting anybody go once they've got their hands on someone." Dig turned to Sky. "And you were standing right beside him during all this?"

Sky shrugged. "I don't understand it either. I thought Spindor was going to grab me and put me in the van too, but he never tried."

Dig looked very seriously at Sky. "Is there something you're not telling me? Did he ask you to do anything?"

Sky shook her head. "I thought he might, but he didn't."

"Was he asking a lot of questions?"

"Only about Chip and me."

"What sort of questions?"

"Where we lived, how long we'd been here, that kind of thing."

Dig nodded knowingly. "Aha, that might explain everything. I bet he's trying to turn you into an informer.

"But the questions were all stuff about us, nobody else. Just chatting really."

"Yes, that's often how it starts, to gain your confidence but the next time you meet . . . Did he suggest another meeting?"

"No. The opposite in fact, he said he never, ever, wanted to see either of us again."

There was a knock on the door and Guts thrust his head inside the hut. "Are you coming, or what? There's people waiting to get started building this hut and I'm starving!"

Twelve

After a slow start, while Dig painstakingly set up four all-important corner posts on which everything else depended, the hut progressed quite quickly. Because it wasn't large enough to fill the whole site, people were able to work in pairs on all four sides at once, without getting in each other's way.

While Guts and Buzz worked on the front wall, Dig and Chip concentrated on making a really sturdy door which would eventually be attached by some splendid wrought-iron hinges that Dig had illegally removed from an Outsider's yard gate.

For most people the prospect of food was what encouraged them to get the work done. Sky, who danced round all evening getting in everybody's way, had craftily decided, so that people wouldn't just eat and then slope off, that they'd break for food around sunset, by which time she hoped the walls would be finished.

Only Guts had objected. "I bet it's all a con and there's nothing but old rags, or something, in them carrier bags."

"There!" Sky opened the bag of cakes right under Guts' nose to prove it.

Guts couldn't believe his luck. "Cor! Can I try one?"

Sky snapped the bag shut. "Not until the work's done."

"But I haven't eaten all day," Guts whined.

"Oh, yes," Sky laughed, "you look as if you might fade away any minute."

"Just one?" Guts went on and on. "Just one to get me going?"

At last Sky had relented and handed everybody one cake. "But there's no more until the sun disappears behind the Tip."

Not a great crowd turned up. Apart from Dig, Sky, Chip and Guts, as expected, Childie and Berry were waiting to help them, though poor Berry had had to bring Popcorn and July with her, who got into everything. Buzz was there and the boy who lived next door, Famous Pinhead.

It was obvious how he got the name Pinhead, but his first name aroused Sky's curiosity. "What's he famous for?" she whispered to Dig.

Dig laughed. "That's the whole point, nobody knows! But at least they keep talking about him, if only to ask how he got his name, so I suppose in a way he is famous."

Though quite a crowd, including a group of lads, their heads frazzled with glue-sniffing, stopped to watch, probably hoping for a free handout, the only other person to offer help was Jeans, who worked, with the exception of Dig, harder than anyone.

"I don't remember seeing him before," Sky said to Berry.

"No, Jeans has only just come back to the Tip. He's been staying in one of those orphanages I told you about."

The idea that anyone should want to give up having a real roof over their heads and being given three proper meals a day, without having to constantly scavenge and live in fear of their lives, astonished Sky. "But if he was lucky enough to get a place, why on earth did he give it up?"

"Ask Jeans," Berry said and rushed off to stop Popcorn pushing precious nails into the ground.

As the light began to fade, Dig lit the bonfire and Childie popped in a few potatoes she'd found, to cook while they worked.

Jeans sighed when Sky first put the question to him, almost as if he couldn't understand his own actions either. "You haven't been here long, Sky, but I bet already there are plenty of things you either do, or maybe don't do, that you wouldn't be allowed to get away with when you were living with grown-ups."

Remembering the cleanliness her mother had insisted on and looking at the sorry state of Chip's clothes after a day's Picking, Sky nodded.

"Here you please yourself what you do," Jeans explained, as he continued to nail a length of wood on to the back of the hut. "What you eat, when you get up and go to bed, even whether to go to work, or not to bother, that's all up to you. You've got freedom of choice."

"You call this freedom?" Sky smiled round the shanty-town. "Free to starve to death, or die of disease, maybe, but sometimes here I feel more trapped, more of a prisoner than if I really was locked up in a prison cell. And yet, if I set foot off the Tip I run the risk of immediately being snapped up by the Catchers!"

"Yes, I know what you mean," Jeans agreed, "but I've been living here for three years and it's what I'm used to. The orphanages are nothing like this. They're rigid, cold places. I mean, nobody comes round tucking you in at night there either and although you're always surrounded by people, there's no privacy, you're still on your own, if you catch my drift. Here, if you don't happen to like somebody you can always stay out of their way, but not if you're

100

stuck in the same dormitory, have to eat with them, do lessons with them. There's nowhere to hide. You can't escape them. Which is how fights break out!"

"Is that what happened to you?"

Jeans nodded. "The monks are very strict and if you break any rules, even getting up five minutes late, you get punished. You can imagine what happens if you rearrange somebody's face! Mind you, I'm used to being thrashed. My dad beat me up something rotten. Which is why I ran away from home in the first place. So when you've been living outside the system as long as I have, it isn't easy to go back to all that discipline. Pass me that other piece of wood."

Sky handed it to him. "But didn't you know what it would be like before you went into the orphanage?"

"Oh, yes, this is the second time I've been in one of those places." Jeans slowly shook his head as he thought about his experience. "I was really determined to stick to it this time, 'cos they got one thing I need in there, education." Jeans looked embarrassed. "You see, I quit school when I was six and I can't read or write. If I don't get myself a dose of education soon I'm going to be stuck here for the rest of my life and I don't want that!"

Sky remembered her own attempts to encourage Chip to learn, using anything which came to hand, old newspapers, or comics she'd found in trash cans. But after a heavy day's work he was frequently too tired to take in much. But Chip's progress wasn't helped by not being able to understand how it would help him get a job. "I'm already earning a living. Anyway, Dad could do all that stuff," Chip had grumbled, "and it didn't do him any good, did it?"

"Jeans, you really ought to give it one more go."

"I know all that! I'm a good worker with my hands, but I'll never get nowhere if I can't at least read and do sums. Trouble is, I think I've left it too late." The hammer lay idle, weighing down his hand, as Jeans considered his future.

"Maybe I could help," Sky suggested.

"Oh, you've got your own problems."

"One of which is trying to teach Chip," Sky said. "I could just as easily do you both at once. In fact, you being there might encourage Chip."

Jeans' eyes brightened. "You mean it?"

"I promise," Sky smiled, "as soon as we're settled in here."

"Right!" said Jeans, and he began to hammer away even harder.

"Time for food!" Guts declared, dropping his hammer the second the last red segment of the sun sank behind the Tip.

"Cakes! Cakes!" Popcorn and July shouted in chorus.

Not only were the walls up, as Sky had hoped, but most of the roof was on too. "We've only got the roof to cover with plastic sheet and the door to fix on and it'll be finished," she said. "So we might just as well do that before we eat."

Even Dig joined in that chorus of protest. "No way! I'm tired, thirsty and hungry. My back aches and I want to sit down before I hit another nail."

"Only joking," Sky lied and produced the bags of food.

Berry laid an old cloth on the ground and the children promptly sat beside it. "And I thought we might be needing these," Berry said and produced two large bottles of deep red liquid.

Guts licked his lips. "Some of your special brew?"

"Special brew?" Sky asked. "What is it?"

Dig flopped down and uncorked one of the bottles. "It's no good asking, she'll never tell." Berry smiled a secretive, but flattered smile. "All she's ever told us is, it's made from the flowers and berries which grow wild round here. And, of course, it's how she got her name. Try some," Dig said, passing it to Sky, "before I'm tempted to drink the whole bottle."

Sky put her lips to the mouth of the bottle and cautiously tipped the contents. As the cordial trickled over her tongue a blissful look spread across her face. Sky truly thought Berry's mystic recipe seemed to contain the very essence of her own lost, forgotten childhood. The bitter-sweet taste captured in a bottle all those half-forgotten flavours and brought back memories of sunny days, with Mum bathing Sky's grazed knees in their own garden.

If Guts hadn't cried out, "Hey, leave some for us!" she might never have stopped drinking and when she handed the bottle along there were tears in her eyes.

"What's up with you?" Chip asked.

Sky knew she couldn't explain, he would either recognise it for himself, or perhaps not. "Nothing," she said putting a hand over his. "I'm tired, that's all."

Childie, who'd been raking through the embers of the fire, re-joined the group. "Who wants a jacket potato?"

When most of the food had gone and they'd all eaten better than anyone could remember, they lay back with only the softest red glow from the fire lighting their faces.

"That was the best picnic I've ever had!" Dig said wistfully.

"Yeh!" Buzz and Jeans agreed.

Guts was wondering if he could stuff in just one more bread roll, but even he had to admit defeat. "I couldn't eat another thing." He said it so soulfully that everybody laughed at him.

Darkness fell. Popcorn and July were asleep, their heads in Berry's lap, while the older children lay on their backs gazing up at the twinkling stars in the black velvet sky.

Jeans voiced all their thoughts when he said, "I wouldn't mind finding a jewel box like that on the Tip!"

Buzz abruptly sat up. "Hey, that reminds me, it was in the papers tonight. Some rich old girl's gone and lost her diamond tiara. Worth thousands, so it said. They've offered a big reward to try and get it back."

"Lost it?" Berry said, her voice heavy with scorn. "If she's that careless she didn't deserve to have it in the first place, let alone get it back again!"

"Thing is," Buzz went on, "it might turn up on the Tip."

Sky smiled. "Turn up here?"

"Come on, Buzz!" Dig laughed. "That's every Picker's daydream. We're all out there fooling ourselves that one day we'll make a big find, the one big enough to get us off the Tip for ever."

"Yes, but it could happen," Buzz said. "It said in the paper that this rich old bird had hidden it in a wastepaper basket . . ."

"She what?"

"Yes, she usually keeps it in the bank, but they went out to this big election dinner and got back late. She was frightened of burglars, so she hid it in the wastepaper basket and by the time she woke up in the morning everything had been emptied and the rubbish collected. So it could be lying out on the Tip right now!"

"I tell you one thing, if I find it I won't give it her back, reward or no reward," Guts said. "Not something worth all that much. I'd sell it."

But Dig shook his head. "You couldn't do that."

"Why not?"

"Something that's been seen in all the papers?" Dig

scoffed. "No Fence would touch it and if they did, they'd probably give you less than the reward and then claim that for themselves."

Guts grabbed another roll and said, spluttering through the crumbs, "I'm still going to look for it!"

"What would you do with the money if you found it?" Jeans asked.

"Easy," Guts replied. "The first thing I'd do is buy myself some new clothes, then I'd go to one of those sauna places and get myself all cleaned up."

Sky smiled. "That's a surprise!"

"And then I'd visit the best restaurant in town and have the biggest meal they'd got!"

Everybody laughed. "That sounds more like you," Buzz said. "What about you, Dig?"

Dig thought for a moment, a dreamy look in his eyes. "If there was enough money I'd buy a little house out in the country, miles from anywhere and I'd grow all my own food so that I'd never have to come back into the city again."

Most people murmured their agreement, but Sky couldn't help wishing that he'd left room in his plan for her. These days Dig seemed very anxious to get rid of them.

The first hint of the moon appeared. It rose swiftly until a bright, golden disc hung in the sky.

Dig jumped up. "Well, we'd better get this hut finished and go to bed, or none of us will be up to Pick anything tomorrow!"

Berry eased up the sleepy figures of Popcorn and July, who rubbed their eyes. "I think these two ought to be in bed right now," she said.

"No!" they both protested. "We want to stay."

"Hush a minute!"

"What is it?" Sky asked.

"Ssh!"

At first all Sky could hear above the usual distant

105

murmur of city traffic was the clatter of trucks being shunted up in the yard and the splash of waves on the shore. Then, closer too, she heard the noise of car engines accompanied by raucous shouts and catcalls.

"Look!" Jeans pointed out into the darkness.

Some distance away Sky spotted several pairs of headlights heading at speed towards them. They were moving in a line along the beach right down by the water's edge. As they raced along the beach, by the lights of the other vehicles, they saw that the leading car's wheels were sending up great arcs of spray which fell on the passengers in the open-topped beach buggies behind and soaked them.

"Oh, no!" Guts groaned. "Not them again."

"Buzz!" Dig said urgently. "Go and hit the drum." As Buzz ran off he turned to Berry. "You and Childie get the little kids out of the way. Chip, you'd better go with them."

"I'm not a little kid," Chip protested.

But Dig was in no mood for argument. "Do what you're told." Cowed, Chip went. "Come on, everybody!"

"What's going on?" Sky asked, as everyone headed for the square. "Who are they?"

The noise of the rapidly beaten oil drum thumped out over the darkened shanties and sleepy heads popped out of doors.

"Hooligans from the city," Dig shouted above the general hubbub of people. "Rich kids who stuff themselves with drink and drugs and get a kick out of making a nuisance of themselves."

"What are we going to do?" she asked.

"Do?" Dig laughed bitterly. "There's nothing except stick together and hope they don't do too much damage."

The roar of the buggies' engines and the drunken shouts of their occupants were getting louder. The

106

crowd of children, silent now, huddled together in the square and, looking out over the roofs of the huts, watched powerless, as the blazing lights drew closer.

The vehicles seemed to slow down briefly on the edge of the encampment, close to where Sky and Chip's hut was being built, before accelerating again. Suddenly there was a sharp crack of splintering wood as the leading buggy hit the first hut and the flimsy structure collapsed beneath its wheels like a cigarette packet.

"Oh, no! They can't!" Sky cried out.

The other vehicles had spread out and were also driving recklessly through the camp as effectively as a corps of tanks, flattening everything in their path. Anything which remained upright was shoved along by the buggies' front bumpers and used as an even more devastating battering ram against the next hut.

So much junk piled up in front of one buggy that it was brought to a juddering halt, engine roaring, wheels spinning. The drunken passengers, who were standing up and being thrown about as they held on to the roll bar, laughed and shouted encouragement at the driver. He reversed and rammed the pile several times before he successfully forced his way through, to the accompaniment of mocking cheers, and ploughed into several more huts.

"Isn't there anything we can do?" Sky whispered to Dig.

He stood, like the other Pickers, silently watching their homes being destroyed as one side of the camp was ripped apart. "Nothing. It isn't just huts they flatten. These people make the Catchers look like pushovers. They're so crazy they'd kill anybody who gets in their way. Just drive straight over them."

Finally the leading vehicle screeched to a halt on the edge of the square, just in front of the crowd and the driver, a boy of about seventeen with black, slicked-back hair and wild, dark eyes, stood up. "Hey, scum! he shouted at them. We've come to bring one of your friends back home."

"Yes," one of his cronies shouted. "She said she wanted a lift!"

From the back of the buggy, two people tossed up in the air a half-naked, bloodstained body.

From the only garment on the body, a ripped, red satin skirt, Sky knew at once that it was Cherry.

For a second the body hung in midair; hair, arms and legs flapping as if they were parts of a weak bird making a feeble attempt at flight. Then the body plummeted into a crumpled heap on the earth.

"Take care of yourselves, scum!" the driver shouted and with a whoop he turned his buggy in a crazy circle, narrowly missing the still figure lying on the ground, and roared off, back the way he'd come.

The moment the vehicles left everyone ran towards the body. Dig, one of the first to reach it, stopped Sky. "Don't look. It's horrible."

"It is Cherry, isn't it?"

Dig nodded. "There are stab wounds all over her body." He looked up at the departing red rear lights of the buggies as they bumped over the remains of the outskirts of the camp. "Bastards!" he screamed after them.

And for the very first time, Sky saw tears in his eyes.

"We're holding this Cleansing for Cherry," Berry began in a steady voice. "She was one of the kindest people, who took nothing for herself, but would always generously help others, sharing what little she had with them. If she had a fault, it was that she did not take enough care of herself. The way we're forced to live involves risk. Perhaps good might come

108

from what's happened to Cherry, because it should remind us all to keep those risks as small as possible."

The gathering of everyone from the shanty-town on the beach, some metres beyond the broken edges of camp, had been timed to coincide with the turning of High Tide.

They all stood, barefoot, in a wide semicircle around the body of Cherry; Berry by her head and Childie at her feet.

During the night several girls had taken away Cherry's body and bathed her, removing all traces of the blood. Once dry, she had been slipped gently into an empty, white flour sack which was tied round her neck, so that only her head was visible.

Sky couldn't help thinking how pathetically young Cherry looked, lying there, eyes closed as if she slept, without her usual garish make-up, her hair neatly brushed and tied back with a ribbon. And also how innocent.

She thought it was too easy to forget, perhaps because of the strength they showed in facing up to the tough life they endured, that all the people gathered there, including herself, were merely children.

Cherry's body lay on a narrow raft built by Dig and Jeans.

"At least, this time, there'll be no shortage of wood," Dig had said grimly, as they set off to search the ruins of the demolished huts for useful spars.

Water lapped gently at the raft which was buoyed up by sealed tin cans, plastic bottles, inflated plastic bags, anything that would hold air. The whole of the raft, around the body, was strewn with yellow, red and blue wild flowers the Pickers had brought. So many that the air was heady with their perfume.

Berry and Childie, holding on to either end of the raft, slowly waded out into the water. They were

109

waist deep with the raft rocking gently on the waves before Berry continued.

"Cherry, with all our love, we start you now on your last journey to meet your own particular God. Go, knowing that you will never be forgotten, but will live for ever in the memories of all those here."

While Berry and Childie swam further out to sea, towing the raft, everyone on the beach shed their clothes and waded in until each one was covered to the neck.

They began the ritual of washing, which Dig had explained to Sky was an important part of any Cleansing.

"So far as I know, it's always happened when somebody from the Tip dies. The only alternative would be to leave her body on the street for one of the Meat Wagons to pick up. We'd rather have the Cleansing."

"Why is it called that?"

"Cherry's death was different, but often we don't know what kills any of us, so the Cleansing is as much for our own protection, in the hope that we'll get rid of any germs.

"But shouldn't you go to the police? Cherry was brutally murdered." Sky's fierce desire for revenge against the Hooligans arose partially from Cherry's death, but also from the callous demolition of so many huts, including their new one, which they'd worked so hard to complete.

"I'm sure they'd be delighted to hear the news that there's another street kid they won't have to bother about. No, Sky, all we've got is the Cleansing. It's only a small thing, I know, but you'll see, it helps us feel a little better."

Once immersed in the water they used any kind of soap they had, from tiny scraps of heavily perfumed

110

toilet soap, to cups of washing-up liquid, or plain ordinary soap powder.

When they had thoroughly cleaned their bodies, they turned and washed their neighbours' hair. Finally rinsing out the soap by completely submerging themselves beneath the water. Some, never having been taught to swim, were very careful.

Afterwards, as they lay on the hot sand, drying themselves in the sun, Sky felt a kind of peace coming over her.

Dig had been right. Though the Cleansing hadn't taken away the horror and fear she'd felt over what had happened to Cherry, somehow the rituals had soothed some of the pain. She realised this was due to them all being present, even Dozer. So that the deep emotions they all felt became a shared experience and nobody was left to suffer them alone in their hut.

They watched silently, while the ebbing tide gently carried away the raft and the white foam of soap they'd left. Not until the raft had turned into a tiny dot and it had eventually disappeared from sight did anyone start to dress and leave the beach.

"What happens now?" Sky asked, as they all trailed back in a long line towards the camp.

"We keep on going, what else?" Dig replied.

"I meant about the huts."

"They'll have to be rebuilt, of course. This isn't the first time since I've been here that something like this has happened. Besides, there's no choice, is there?"

"No," Sky said, but she felt she lacked the inner spark that always, whatever the crisis, seemed to propel Dig and the others onwards. Sky doubted she had the mental, let alone physical, strength to survive life on the Tip. Yet although she knew there had

111

to be an alternative way of life, she didn't know what it was.

As she gazed out to sea, Sky couldn't help remembering the bloody, butchered corpse the Hooligans had dropped to the ground in front of them and she shuddered when she thought that, if she didn't do something soon, her own life might end in a similarly abrupt and hideous fashion.

Thirteen

Soon after the Cleansing, Sky and Chip, after a good deal of argument on Sky's part, had moved into Cherry's old hut.

When Dig had first suggested the idea, Sky wouldn't hear of it. "I couldn't! I just couldn't!"

Dig had patiently tried to reason with her. "Surely not because of the murder?"

"No," she lied, "of course not."

"Because Cherry didn't die anywhere near her hut."

"I know, Dig, but all the same . . ."

"You also know she didn't do any of her work there either, the hut was simply where she lived."

"I understand all that."

"And there are plenty of other people, whose huts got flattened by the Hooligans, who'd jump at the chance and with all the other huts to rebuild it could be a while before you get another."

"I'd rather wait," Sky said frankly, "but I suppose you want us out."

"No, it isn't that." Dig tried to sound casual. "It just seems a shame not to be using all the furniture and stuff you'd collected."

Sky had been feeling guilty about all their bits and pieces cluttering up Dig's hut.

"The sooner you and Chip have a place of your own, the quicker you'll begin to feel part of the place. I think you at least ought to go and look at the hut."

Sky couldn't find a way to tell Dig that feeling "part of the place" was the last thing she wanted – less than ever after what the Hooligans had done to Cherry. So they went, but Sky had started to find fault with everything even before they went inside. "The building slopes down at one end."

"Erosion caused by the rain we had. I could probably do something about that," Dig calmly replied. "It's mostly one huge wooden packing case. Heaven knows how it got here, but we could get some help to lift up one side and stick some rocks underneath to level it up." With difficulty he opened the rickety door which hung from a single hinge made from a strip of cloth. He said quickly, before Sky had time to complain, "I rescued the hinges from your old door."

Once inside, it wasn't the grubby blanket, carelessly tossed aside on to the floor, the unwashed cup and plate, or even the mouse that scuttled into a corner as they opened the door, which really put Sky off. It was the smell of the cheap scent Cherry always wore, which seemed to Sky to hang in the air all around her like a thick mist.

Dig didn't notice. Practical as ever, he was far too busy examining the structure; banging on the walls and stamping on floorboards. "Not many places have a proper floor," he pointed out.

"But it's soaking wet."

"True, but most of that'll go away once we've levelled the place up and then, on the top side, we can dig a drainage trench to stop that happening again." He could see Sky still wasn't happy. "Look, Sky, I know it doesn't look much as it is now, but you don't have to come here again until Chip and I have cleaned the whole thing out. You'll see, it'll be a different place then and this way you won't have to wait ages, collecting all that wood again, to build something new. And there's one other thing."

114

"Oh, what?"

"Here you'd be quite near the top of the site. There's no way the Hooligans could get near it."

That argument finally clinched the deal. Although the hut was nearer the Tip, so the smell was much stronger, night after night Sky had been having dreadful, scary nightmares about the Hooligans returning. Their buggies would crash through the wall beside her and the horrible boy with slicked-back hair tied her up and carried her off into the night with him.

"Okay," she agreed reluctantly.

But even after Dig and Chip had removed all of Cherry's possessions and, while it was empty, had scrubbed the whole place from top to bottom, Sky was convinced the smell of the scent remained, as if the wooden walls had absorbed it.

But she'd never mentioned that, not even to Chip, and once they'd moved in their own belongings it began to feel a little better. Except, of course, that they were not really *their* things, but other people's cast-offs.

Friends visiting made Sky more comfortable. Berry often came and Sky kept her promise to Jeans, about teaching him to read and write. Word quickly spread around the camp about those lessons and around the time they were due, after the evening meal, so many other children drifted by to listen and look over shoulders, they were forced to work outside.

But Dig wasn't one of them.

Chip still saw him while working on the Tip but, because she avoided going there, Sky didn't. There had been many things about Dig which annoyed her, not least of all his habit of almost always turning out to be right about things, but now she hardly saw him, she missed his company and his sensible advice.

They still bumped into each other around the camp,

but Dig never seemed inclined to stop and talk. He'd wave to her, or say hello, but keep on walking. That hurt and if she happened to catch sight of him talking to Childie, or merely walking along with Berry, Sky was very jealous. Sometimes she regretted falling out over Tiny.

While they were still living with Dig, Sky had planned to give him some kind of thank-you present when they left. After much discussion, Chip had suggested making the hand-cart Dig was always saying he wanted. In a rubbish skip in the city, Chip found a pair of old pram wheels. He'd also got two long, thin lengths of wood for the handles. He'd built a body out of old fruit boxes and painted the whole cart. Because the paint was only drops left in the bottoms of tins he hadn't been able to find enough of one colour to do the whole thing, so each side had come out as several different colours.

In a way Sky thought the "patchwork" look added to its novelty and it still looked very smart and new. It even had "Dig" painted on the front in white letters, though the G had run a little.

But it stayed behind the hut, covered with a piece of torn sheet, because Sky was no longer certain she wanted to give Dig anything. Some of her gratitude had evaporated and she was beginning to seriously think about keeping it for themselves.

They'd been living in what Sky still regarded as Cherry's hut for about three months when one morning she happened to be collecting water from the standpipe as Dozer ambled up carrying a plastic bottle.

Lately Dozer hadn't shown the slightest intention of carrying out any of his threats against Dig, or herself, but just having him standing beside her made the hairs on the back of her neck prickle.

116

But instead of ignoring her as usual, he opened up a conversation. "How are you making out now?"

"Okay," she cautiously replied.

"Happy in the place you've got?" Dozer asked.

That was a bit near the mark! "It's okay."

"So, what do you do all day? I never see you on the Tip."

"Chip goes."

"Yes, I've seen him, but what do you do?" he asked, innocently opening up a rich vein of guilt in Sky.

The fact was, because she hated the Tip she did nothing beyond cooking, washing and mending. Bearing in mind how little food they managed on and how few clothes they had, that didn't amount to much. Truth to tell she was starting to feel like a millstone round Chip's neck and she was beginning to think he'd probably be better off without her around. He was a great Picker and well able to look after himself now.

"I've been thinking about getting a job," she said and blushed. "Maybe something like Buzz, selling papers."

Dozer brightened up. "I might be able to help you there."

"I'm not working for you, Dozer!"

He actually laughed! Sky didn't think she'd seen him so much as smile before and it was not a pretty sight.

"I think you're a bit big to be a Ferret!" he said. "No, this is a place that's got some jobs going. I happen to know the man who runs it, guy called Beacon, and he said I should mention it around the Tip. He said the pay's okay."

"For doing what exactly?"

Dozer shook his head. "I don't know much about it, not my scene. But I've scribbled the address down, you should go and have a chat with Beacon."

Sky took the scrap of paper, but Dozer having it all written out ready kept her suspicions aroused. "And what do you get out of this, Dozer?"

"Me?" Dozer's eyebrows shot up in astonished innocence. "Nothing, why?"

"People like you don't do anything for nothing! It wasn't long ago you threatened to 'get' me, remember?"

"Oh, Sky, that was a long time ago. Anyway, please yourself. It doesn't bother me whether you go, or not. If the pay's as good as he says, the jobs have probably already gone."

Sky glanced at the piece of paper and stuffed it into her pocket, but the idea nagged at her for the rest of the day and the following morning, without a word to anyone, she decided there would be no harm in having a look.

The address was on the far side of town in a district Sky didn't know very well. To reach it she had to pass through a smart residential area. Broad, tree-lined roads were flanked by large, white detached houses with huge gardens.

She was walking down the side of one of these, alongside a high, white wall, when she came to a tall, wrought-iron gate. Clutching the bars, Sky peered into the garden. Apart from the green bushes and beautiful flowers, Sky could see a fountain splashing water into a large, circular stone fish pond. Hot and dusty, she longed to trail her hands through that cool, sparkling water.

Beyond the pool, Sky saw an elegant wooden summerhouse built in the style of a Buddhist pagoda. Then she noticed a girl sitting within its cool shade. She looked about Sky's age and had long dark hair. She wore a crisp white skirt with a dark blue blouse and was busy writing.

Sky, her head now pressed against the bars of the gate, couldn't help wishing she was that girl. How wonderful it must be, she thought, to live safe within the protection of those high walls, in a large house, and have such a beautiful, quiet garden. To be able to sit in the shade and have nothing more pressing to do than write.

Just then the girl glanced up and saw Sky staring at her. For a second their eyes met, held each other and Sky smiled shyly, but the girl let out a scream and ran up the garden towards the house shouting, "Mummy! Mummy! There's a beggar at the gate!"

Sky ran off, feeling hurt and yet indignant about the girl's low opinion of her. Sky believed, only a year ago, that same girl might possibly have invited her in, or at least talked to her through the gate but she would never have been treated as an untouchable, an object of fear.

Perhaps it was the girl's reaction which made Sky more determined than ever to find a way of changing her life. At first when she couldn't find the address on the piece of paper, she'd thought of abandoning the search. Now, she persisted in asking people for directions and though she was careful, after her experience with the rich girl in the garden, what sort of people she asked, she was increasingly aware that they too gave her strange looks.

"Maybe I really do look like a beggar now," she thought.

At long last she found the street. Dozer calling it a factory had given her an image of large buildings, but this was a dreary street of big, old houses, many of which were as run down as the ones around the Jungle.

Several small firms had set up business in them, often as many as four different ones in the same house. From many came the constant hum of machinery. Somebody was hammering metal in one, while from a second came the loud whirr of industrial sewing machines.

On the slightly sunnier side of the dismal street, people sat on the stone steps and, with no particular interest, watched her pass as she searched the name boards displayed by the doors.

The place she was looking for turned out to be at the far end of the street; a tall, thin house which seemed to have been squashed by the high brick wall that blocked off the end of the street. No sound came from the house, though there was a rather curious smell which burned Sky's eyes, making them water.

A fat, bald-headed man sat on the steps, counting a thick roll of money which he hastily thrust into a back pocket when Sky's shadow fell across him.

"Are you Beacon?" she asked.

"Who needs to know?"

"I'm Sky."

"Oh, yeah?" Beacon said suspiciously.

"Dozer, from the Tip, sent me."

The man's face lightened a little. "Oh, yeah?"

"He said you might have some work for me."

"Work? How old are you?"

"Thirteen," she lied, realising it was getting to be a habit.

"You know perfectly well, if you under sixteen I can't give you no work," Beacon said.

"But Dozer said . . ."

"I don't care what Dozer said! I ain't gonna break no law. They could throw me in jail for that."

"Oh," was the best Sky could manage. She'd trailed all this way for nothing.

Sky started to walk off, but she'd only gone a couple of steps when Beacon called her back. "Here, little girl, not so fast. I don't like to see you goin' off lookin' so miserable."

"We need the money," Sky said.

"Don't we all?"

Sky wondered why he said that when moments earlier she'd seen him busily counting so much of his.

"Can't buy you everything, money can't, but it sure do make the waitin' pleasanter!" Beacon looked furtively up the street. He stood up, moved closer to Sky and whispered. "You any good at keepin' secrets?"

"Yes."

But then he appeared to change his mind. "Oh, I don't know. You're very young and I can see myself gettin' in bother."

"I won't tell anybody anything," she promised eagerly.

"Well," Beacon began, slowly, "it just happens, I might have an openin' for a bright girl like you."

"Oh, that'd be great."

"If I'm any judge, you look like a pretty good worker to me."

"I am, honestly."

"Well, let's not hang about out here, where everybody can mind our business. If you're from the Tip you had a long walk . . . Maybe we should go inside and discuss this over a nice drink of iced water. How does that sound?"

Sky nodded. "That sounds great."

"Okay, little girl, you come with me."

Sky had only followed Beacon halfway up the steps when, from behind, a hand dropped on her shoulder. "Not so fast," a voice said.

Sky spun round and found herself looking into the dark brown eyes of Spindor.

Fourteen

"What business is this of yours, mister?" Beacon snarled.

Sky, who was no more pleased by the interruption than Beacon was, glared at Spindor, who didn't appear to notice.

"I intend to make it my business," Spindor said casually. He wasn't in uniform but wore lightweight slacks and a putty-coloured shirt. He flicked open his wallet and pulled out an identity card which he thrust under Beacon's prominent nose. "I'm from the Child Protection Unit."

"Oh, I see," Beacon said, looking relieved. "You're after a pay-off. You Catchers is all alike. Well, you're out of luck. She came of her own accord, on somebody else's say so. I ain't payin' you anythin' for this one."

"That's right," Sky said. "I want to earn some money to get off the Tip, like you said, and someone told me I could get a job here."

Spindor smiled, a twisted kind of smile. "Oh, you'll get off the Tip all right if you work for Beacon! In fact you'll probably never see it, or the light of day again."

"You've no cause to go interferin'!" Beacon snapped.

"Yes I have. Says right here on this card that it 'gives right of access at all times to private premises where it is believed a minor may be endangered'."

Beacon laughed. "I've never before heard of a Catcher doing anythin' about it though."

"And I'm not in danger," Sky added.

"Yes, you are," Spindor said without looking at her, "greater than you realise."

"Look, I can't stand around all day arguin' with you," Beacon said, heading for the door. "Little lady, you either want the job, or you're goin' to stand around listenin' to him. Which is it to be?"

"I want the job," Sky said firmly and she began to follow Beacon up the steps until Spindor stopped her.

"I tell you what, Sky," Spindor said, "why don't we take a look around this place, like my card entitles me to? Then if you still want the job, you can take it."

Beacon flushed. "It's not convenient."

"'At *all* times' it says here." Spindor waved his identity card and smiled one of his slow, easy smiles. "Of course, if you want to prevent me from entering, we could wait for the police to help me get inside."

Sky didn't want that at all, nor apparently did Beacon. "Okay, okay, but make it snappy," he said. "I don't want production disturbed!"

Spindor laughed. "Come on, Sky, an invitation put that pleasantly is irresistible."

"I don't know what all the fuss is about," Sky grumbled.

"That's my whole point!" Spindor replied. "But you soon will."

He tried to take her arm as they walked up the crumbling stone steps, but Sky snatched it away. Why was it that just when something seemed to be going right in her life, he had to come poking his nose in, spoiling everything?

Inside the uncarpeted hall, Beacon headed for the staircase leading to the upper floors, until Spindor called him back. "We're not interested in the offices and storerooms, Beacon. Just take us into the basement where the real work's done. After all, that's where Sky'll be going, if she decides to take the job."

123

Beacon looked very angry. "There ain't nothin' down there!"

"Never mind," Spindor persisted, "we'll take a look anyway." He led the way down the hall and stopped beneath the stairs to open what seemed to be a small cupboard door. As he opened it, the chemical smell that Sky had first noticed outside the house, grew far stronger, making her eyes sting, biting the back of her throat and making her cough.

Beacon didn't follow them down the set of steep, well-worn steps into the gloom of the cellar.

As Sky put out a hand to steady herself she discovered the bricks of the wall were running with damp.

But the sight which awaited her at the foot of the stairs was truly horrifying.

"This is where you'd work," Spindor said quietly.

The room was twenty metres square. It was lit by a single naked bulb which hung by its own flex from a nail driven into the low ceiling. It was helped a little by the small amount of light which managed to penetrate the grime on the narrow ventilator window.

Most of the space in the centre of the cellar was occupied by a large bench, around which sat ten or twelve children. As Sky and Spindor entered all the children, some younger than Chip, but most around her own age, turned to stare at them before going back to work.

The bench was full of heels and soles for shoes which the children were glueing to uppers they took from piles on the floor beside them.

"That smell," Spindor explained, "most of it anyway, apart from the slop bucket in the corner, is the toxic fumes from the glue they use. We're lucky today, the window's open, but in the winter Beacon shuts it and all the fumes are trapped inside."

124

After a little girl pressed a heel and upper together, she wiped off the thin white worm of surplus glue which oozed out with her finger and then automatically cleaned that finger on her jeans.

"That glue dries on their skin," Spindor commented. "It gets in their hair and their eyes. Their clothes get stiff with the stuff. Apart from the kind of skin irritations you might expect, they suffer terrible breathing problems too and eventually many of them end up paralysed. Glue polyneuritis, is its Sunday-go-to-church name. I've known kids who've ended up in hospital and never walked again as a result of working in places like this. Most aren't so lucky, they die and get replaced."

"That's terrible," Sky said with a shudder. "But if it's really as bad as you say, why do these kids do it?"

"Most were sold to Beacon by the Catchers. Not me, I hasten to add! Some, like you, came of their own free will. They've no idea what they're letting themselves in for when they first come here. They're simply attracted by the chance to earn what sounds like easy money. Not that most of them live long enough to collect."

"But once they've seen what it's like, why stay?"

"That's easy." Spindor bent down beside one of the children and lifted up the boy's leg. Around his skinny ankle he wore a shackle on a length of chain which, in turn was fastened to another thicker chain that ran right round the table. "They're a very friendly bunch," Spindor said grimly, "they go everywhere together!"

"You mean they live down here?"

"Night and day. As you're here, you ought to see the luxurious living quarters you'll be sharing with them . . ."

"I've seen enough," Sky protested and tried to leave, but Spindor wouldn't let her.

125

He pushed her through a gap in the wall which divided the cellar into two. The floor of the smaller room was ankle deep in grubby straw. "This is where they eat, what little they get, and sleep."

A rustling sound caught Sky's attention. "What's making those noises?"

"Let me light this candle." Spindor flicked his cigarette lighter.

As the weak light filled the room Sky, to her horror, saw pink-eyed rats turn tail and run off through broken gratings. Then she screamed as something scuttled over her bare foot.

"Don't worry," Spindor said comfortingly. "That wasn't a rat, it was a cockroach."

"Get me out of here!" she demanded.

"Now, hang on," Spindor said, "you were the one who got annoyed with me about getting in the way. You wanted to stay and work here."

Sky, near hysterical, beat his chest with her clenched fists. "Get me out of here, now!"

"But why don't you do something?" Sky demanded. She had calmed down a little but the anger still boiled inside her.

They were sitting at a table outside a small café he'd insisted on taking her to. An untouched milkshake sat in front of Sky. Her stomach for food still hadn't returned!

Spindor sipped his black coffee before answering. "Did you happen to notice there aren't yet any maker's labels in those shoes? Beacon's factory makes them for some famous name or other who puts the labels in later and they sell them for big prices all over the world. That way the shoe firm's reputation stays clean. They'd swear in court, quite truthfully, they had no idea the shoes were made by children and that they knew nothing about the conditions in

126

which they worked. So, in the event of injury or accident the famous shoe company has no legal responsibility, nor has to pay any compensation to any of the victims. That's all down to Beacon, but by the time the trial gets to court, surprise, surprise! Beacon's disappeared."

"But surely you could close that place down now."

"Sure, but he'd open another tomorrow. In different parts of the city, Beacon's got three more basement factories just like that one, and those are just the ones I happen to know about."

"But how can you just sit there, knowing what those children are suffering?"

"In a way that's why I joined the Child Protection Unit in the first place. I'd heard and seen all the terrible things going on around and I believed all the stuff Stin said about the Units and Care Camps being the only answer."

He was speaking so quietly, so they wouldn't be overheard by the other customers, that Sky was forced to lean across the table to hear. "But that's all lies," she hissed.

Spindor nodded and said sadly, "Yes, sure, I know that now." He smiled a wry smile. "When I joined I thought, even if I couldn't change the world, maybe I could make it just a little bit better place, but that's not how things worked out. The whole system's corrupt; half the officers in the Unit have served prison sentences and the other half should. Most of them can be bribed with a stick of gum and they'd shoot their own mother for half that!"

"But you're still a Catcher."

"Hey, now hang on. For a start, I joined in good faith, thinking I could help the street kids."

"But you haven't left now you know better."

"They do have ways of making sure you don't leave."

Sky didn't believe him. "Oh, yes?"

"They get you involved without you realising. I refused to accept the pay-offs my charming partner, Shakey, had arranged, but without me knowing he just paid the money straight into my bank account. When I threatened to leave before the five years I'd signed on for were up, they produced a copy of my bank statement and said, 'How will you explain to the police where all this extra money's come from?'"

"You could have told the truth."

"But they wouldn't have listened. Drugs, that's what the police would have said!"

"And that's your excuse for still getting paid for catching little children and selling them?"

"One: I let you and your brother go when Shakey wasn't there. It's not the first time I've done that but if he knew I'd probably have been found in a dark alley with a bullet through me. Two: I've just bent the rules to rescue you from Beacon's clutches. I'm off duty and Beacon could have hung me out to dry, but when I saw you going down that street I knew what was happening down there and I knew you were going to do something stupid. So I came and rescued you, didn't I?"

Sky grudgingly agreed. "I suppose."

Spindor spread his large hands wide on the table. "Well, then? Listen, whenever I get the chance I do help kids."

"Which must make you feel a lot better," Sky said bitterly, "when you take your blood money."

"I tell you, some kids won't take help when it's offered. Remember how you behaved when I turned up outside Beacon's? They just won't trust me."

"It might have something to do with the uniform you wear and the Catchers' reputation for doing awful things. How do they know you're any different from the rest? I didn't. In fact, I'm still not sure that your kindness isn't part of some even worse scheme."

Spindor smiled. "Ah, you've found me out!"

Sky sat up in alarm. "What?"

"Ssh!" he whispered, glancing over his shoulder. "Listen. I'm determined to put the 'blood money', as you call it, to good use." He broke off and looked at Sky. "I'm not at all sure I should be telling you this. Nowadays I don't know who to trust."

"Me neither," Sky said, "but maybe we already know too much about each other by now, so you might as well risk it."

"I suppose," he said cautiously. "Well, it's like this. My five years as a Catcher are over soon and they can't make me sign on for any longer, but I've collected a tidy amount over those years."

"I bet."

"Just listen, will you? I want to use the money to buy a place, right out in the country, where kids like you, who haven't been corrupted yet, can get away from all this and make a fresh start."

"Places like that already exist, they call them Care Camps, Spindor!"

"This would be different. For a start, nobody would have to go if they didn't want and if they didn't like it, they'd be free to leave at any time. But anybody who stayed would carry on with their education and they'd also have to work to produce the food we'd need."

"Dig would like that," Sky said, it was almost an echo of his dream.

"Who?"

"Dig, just a boy on the Tip who helped us."

"There are some hard cases out there."

"Dig isn't one of them. Just unlucky. He's very kind and helpful."

"And honest?" Spindor asked.

Sky remembered the door hinges he'd stolen for her. "As honest as you and me. He wouldn't harm

129

another human being, but he reckons Outsiders are always fair game."

But Spindor wasn't listening, he was more concerned with his dream. "It's just a question of finding the right people to take. I thought you and your brother . . ."

"Chip."

"Yes, Chip. You two would stand much more chance if you were growing up away from all the pressures and temptations of the city."

"Why not take those kids from Beacon's factory?"

Spindor shook his head. "No, it's too late for them. They're beyond help."

"Yes, well, it's all pie in the sky, isn't it?"

"Oh, no." Spindor lowered his voice even further. "I've found the right place and bought it, miles from here, where they'll never find us." Spindor leaned closer. "But you really mustn't breathe a word about this to anyone."

Sky began to think Spindor might be telling the truth. "I promise."

"Especially your brother, he's too young to understand the full implications."

"Yes, all right! I've said, I promise."

"I'm leaving in a month. What about it? Would you two both like to come?"

Fifteen

"You're not very talkative," Dig complained. "I haven't really seen you for weeks and when I do come, you've nothing to say."

"I'm sorry," Sky apologised. "I've got a lot on my mind." She'd returned, her head whirling with confused thoughts about Beacon's hideous factory. But mainly she was troubled by Spindor's plans. Chip had brought Dig home from the Tip with him.

"Maybe I should come back some other time," Dig suggested.

"No," Sky said hastily. She desperately needed to talk. She realised that in some ways the choice facing her was similar to the ones her parents had faced and she was determined to make a better job of sorting everything out than they had. But how could she ask Dig's advice without breaking her promise to Spindor? A street kid giving a promise to a Catcher, that was a laugh! "I'm sorry, we haven't got much to eat," she said.

"I'm not really hungry," Dig replied politely.

Why had everything between them become so awkward? They'd lived happily together in the same hut for weeks. "What I meant was, there's a sort of vegetable soup I'm going to heat up. You must share that with us." She lit the stove and put on the can containing a thick vegetable soup which she'd concocted from leftovers.

"Okay, whatever."

Chip sensing, though not understanding, the uneasy atmosphere, turned to his original reason for bringing Dig back with him. "We've got a present for you."

He ran out of the hut leaving Dig looking baffled. "A present?"

"Oh, it's nothing . . ." Sky said.

When Chip returned he couldn't get the cart, still covered with the sheet, through the door and so they all trooped outside.

"It's just something we wanted to give you, to repay you for all the help you gave us," Sky said quietly.

"Hey, you shouldn't have bothered," Dig protested with an embarrassed grin.

Chip whipped off the sheet with a fanfare. "Tarrah!"

Dig stepped back. "That's fantastic!"

"Chip found the wheels and did most of the work. I helped with the painting and I put your name on the front so that nobody could pinch it."

"Yes," Chip said, putting his head on one side to give the lettering a critical examination, "you can see where it's run."

Dig still hadn't recovered his usual cool. "I don't know what to say. You really didn't have to do this."

"But we wanted to," Sky said. Having Dig around again and the obvious pleasure he showed at being given the hand-cart made Sky begin to feel better. "You didn't have to look after us the way you did. Think of it as an early birthday present."

"I almost can't remember when I last had one of those," Dig said, looking wistful.

"It's funny," Sky said, "the birthday presents which most stick out in my mind are two of the things we lost when they took the car. My hairbrush and a harmonica I used to play."

132

"I was going to get a bike for my next birthday," Chip said quietly.

"Let's eat, I'm starving," Sky cut in before everybody started getting nostalgic, which usually led directly to depression.

After that the evening went fairly well. Dig was so taken with his cart that they ate outside, so he could keep on admiring it.

But Spindor was still uppermost in her thoughts so, while Chip had gone for water, when Dig said he thought he ought to go, Sky insisted on walking back with him.

"You know you've always wanted to live in the country?" she began, trying to sound casual as they strolled between the rows of huts. "I remember you talking about it the night the Hooligans came."

"Yes."

"Suppose something happened that might make that possible?"

"Oh, come on, Sky!"

"Yes, I know it isn't likely, but just suppose."

"You mean like get sold for adoption to some rich family that lives in the country? Sounds like one of the Catchers' favourite scams."

"No," Sky said, though that set her wondering. "Nothing like that. A straight-up deal to go and live in the country, no strings attached."

Dig smiled. "Things like that just don't happen to kids like us, Sky. Funny, I thought you'd begun to settle down really well, but it's no good clinging on to fantasies like that one, you can drive yourself crazy."

"But if it _could_ be arranged," Sky insisted, "it's what you've always said you wanted to do. Would you go?"

"Yes, I suppose. In the same way as I'd go to the moon and that's just as likely!"

Sky didn't feel she could push the issue any further.

Dig obviously thought the idea so outlandish that he wasn't going to bother to consider it seriously.

Sky didn't go straight home but popped in to talk to Berry. Spindor had suggested that, as she clearly didn't believe him, on his next day off Sky should join him on a trip out to see the place he'd bought. Sky's doubts about going with him included the possibility that Spindor might be intending to kidnap her. Therefore she had to face the possibility of not getting back and who would look after Chip?

Sky found Berry washing out food containers under the standpipe tap. They exchanged scraps of news and then Sky said, "Berry, if anything should happen to me . . ."

Berry looked up from her work, her steady eyes searching Sky's. "What kind of thing?"

"Oh, I don't know, anything," Sky replied evasively.

"You're not sick, are you?" Berry asked.

"No, of course not, but there's nothing very certain about life out here and you said yourself, if anything happened to me there'd be no one to look after Chip. He's still very young, too young to take care of himself in spite of all he's learned here. I'd just like to be sure somebody would be looking out for him."

"Oh, I see!" Berry sighed with relief. "I thought something must be wrong. Either that, or you were planning to go off on your own somewhere."

Sky was always surprised how attuned the ears were of people who lived on the Tip. Living by their wits seemed to sharpen their ears not only to rumour, but the slightest shade of nuance, or change of voice. "No, I wouldn't leave him behind," Sky said firmly, "not from choice anyway, but you can never tell how things will turn out."

"That's the truth," Berry said thoughtfully.

* * *

134

For the next few days Sky wandered round continually sifting every word Spindor had said, trying to discover what dreadful trap lay behind it all. The fact that she couldn't find anything didn't make her mind any easier. Consequently on Spindor's next off-duty day, the day of her trip into the country, Sky made an extra fuss of Chip as he left for the Tip.

"Take care out there, won't you?" she said.

Chip had looked blank. "I always do, what do you mean?"

Sky felt awkward. There was so much she wanted to say, in case she didn't return, but felt she couldn't without giving away what she was doing. In which case he would probably have tried to stop her going, or got Dig to.

"I just meant . . . it's a dangerous place . . . be careful, that's all," she finished, lamely.

But after he'd gone and she was alone in the hut, Sky wished, if this was to be the last she was to see of her brother, that she had at least hugged him, though if she had he would probably have thought she'd gone totally mad.

Her fears grew as she left the camp. As neither Sky nor Spindor were anxious to be seen together, they'd arranged to meet on a patch of waste ground, usually used as a car park, hidden amongst the back streets and alleyways beyond the railway sidings.

All the way there Sky kept glancing over her shoulder to see if anyone was following her. Even when she reached the car park and saw Spindor, sitting waiting in the cab of his white Toyota pick-up truck, she didn't rush straight over to him. Instead she checked around every corner first, convinced that any second a Catchers' van would roll up to carry her away.

Only when Spindor glanced twice at his watch and

then looked as if he were about to drive away without her, thinking she'd changed her mind, did Sky run across the car park.

"Hi, sorry I'm late," she gasped. "I had trouble getting away."

"No problem, hop in," he grinned.

She began to feel more comfortable as they left the city, but there was an awkward moment when she realised they were taking the very road on which their car had finally broken down.

Even after all those months, travelling along that particular road, still so familiar because its image was imprinted for ever in her brain, raised dreadful memories.

Sky desperately felt a desire to push back the hands of the clock, to wind back the film of her life beyond the point at which she'd made her first journey down this road and then run it again, but with a very different ending.

As they drew nearer to the lay-by Sky, straining her eyes against the sun, was startled to see, at the exact spot where their car had been, the figure of her mother, sitting hunched up beside the road, waiting.

"Slow down!" she cried out, gripping Spindor's arm.

Spindor, baffled, applied the brakes. "What's up?"

But then the figure of the woman mysteriously changed back into a large rock marking the bridge over the stream and Sky, disappointed, sank back into her seat. "Nothing," she said, "I thought I saw . . . oh, nothing."

After that shock, and although Sky knew she must keep her wits about her, she found to her surprise that her suspicions were beginning to evaporate. Maybe it was simply the novelty of a day out without having to be constantly on her guard. Spindor was undoubtedly a pleasant, easy companion. As they turned off the main road, which was flanked by arid land, and headed down a cooler, lusher valley of trees, she found the contrast between being out in the countryside and the stark surroundings of the Tip reassuring. Either way, Sky realised she was enjoying herself far more than she'd ever expected.

Three hours after they'd left the city, Spindor slowed down and murmured, "Nearly there." He swung the wheel and they turned off down a narrow, bumpy sandy track.

Sky sat forward eagerly in her seat, trying to catch a first glimpse of this farmhouse which Spindor had described in increasingly idyllic terms throughout the journey.

But she could see nothing except fold upon fold of bushes and trees. Then, just after they'd splashed through the ford of a swift, sparkling stream, sending up an arc of spray which glittered in the sunlight, they rounded a corner and there it was.

Sixteen

Spindor allowed the truck to cruise gradually to a halt, sweeping its way through the waist-high grass which grew in front of the house. He switched off the engine, leaving only the sound of bird song drifting in through the cab's open windows and the air which, after the constant smell of the Tip, tasted like water taken from beneath a fall.

The farmhouse, sunbathing in a clearing in the trees, was old and built from solid blocks of cool, grey stone; their faces softened by the wash of time and partly hidden by the green leaves and purple flowers of a climbing plant which billowed exotically over the walls. It was not the stranglehold of some parasitic plant, more of a loving embrace, or the added beauty of jewellery when worn by an attractive but mature woman.

Though the paint had blistered off the woodwork of the window frames, the glass remained intact, unlike buildings left deserted in the city. A deep verandah ran across half of the front of the house and though, over the years, its floorboards and wooden balustrade had been bleached almost white by the weather, the shade it offered made the whole house seem to welcome them.

"Beautiful, isn't it?" Spindor said quietly, but the beauty silenced Sky. She was afraid to speak in case the spell would be broken and the whole place disappear as swiftly as the morning's sighting of her mother.

"Of course, it'll look a lot better with a coat of paint," Spindor prattled on, "and we'll need to cut all these weeds down."

"Oh, no!" Sky protested. "You can't touch it, it's perfect just the way it is."

Spindor threw his head back and laughed. "It won't be here much longer if we leave it in this state. The windows will fall out and then it'll just crumble away into the weeds! You've got to be practical."

But for the first time for months, Sky felt free of the need to be practical. Where Spindor saw a need for restoration and renewal, Sky found only a sense of permanence, history even, and a solidity that their fragile existence beside the Tip, with its flimsy, makeshift huts, could never offer.

Spindor opened his door and jumped down. "Come on, I've got the key, we can look inside."

Sky reluctantly followed him, convinced that the inside of the house could never live up to the first, breathtaking promise of its exterior.

But it did.

The broad hall, with its wide staircase, led to empty, echoing downstairs rooms which offered more refreshing shade from the heat of the day. Those at the rear looked out over sunlit, blousy, overgrown paddocks fenced with weathered posts and rails.

As he gazed through the window, Spindor sighed with contentment. "Once we get started, there'll easily be enough land out there," Spindor said. "Not only to keep us in food, but to be able to sell some as well for the things we've really got to buy. We should even be able to keep a few animals for milk and meat too."

"Can I look round upstairs?"

"Sure, go ahead, help yourself. I'll be busy down

139

here. I've got some tools in the truck and I want to fix a new lock on the back door."

Having grown used to a cramped hut Sky found the size of the place quite overwhelming at first and although it was quite different from their old home, there was a similar, familiar feel to the cool plaster of its walls which rekindled old memories.

Sky climbed the stairs with their heavily carved banisters and wandered from room to room. As she did she disturbed years of dust; motes hovered, spinning, trapped in brilliant shafts of sunlight.

Initially she moved cautiously, constantly fearing disappointment, but then she began to run around, being continually delighted with each new discovery. Quite simple things pleased her, like being able to peer out over the countryside through the little windows with their overhanging eyebrows of creeper.

But best by far was the huge bathroom. So big, Sky realised, that their entire hut could have been dropped into it without damaging the wall's peeling eggshell blue paintwork.

She loved this room mainly because it contained the largest, deepest bath Sky had ever seen. Beneath the brass mixer tap was a lovely picture, in fading enamel, of a beautiful mermaid with a coiled, silvery tail, her long blonde hair coyly hiding her breasts. She appeared to have swum up through the plughole but then, when the last bathwater had been released, had been left stranded, patiently awaiting the next high tide.

Above the tap, a pipe ran up the white tiled wall to a brass shower head which looked as if it had been taken off a monstrous watering can.

Sky couldn't remember being immersed in water since Cherry's Cleansing and she longed to be able to climb into that tub; to wallow in warm, soapy water right up to her chin. "Not that there's likely to be any water, let alone warm," she mumbled to herself, but she still couldn't resist the temptation to lean over the bath and turn the big brass tap.

Jets of cold water, sharp as needles, shot out of the shower head and caught Sky so much by surprise that she let out a sharp scream.

"Are you okay?" Spindor called up from the foot of the stairs.

"Yes, I'm fine," Sky shouted back. "I was just trying out the shower."

"Really? Are you getting hungry?"

"A bit."

"Good. Well, when you've finished playing around up there, come out into the garden. I've brought some food and we can have a picnic."

"Coming." Sky shook the cold drops of water out of her hair and then caught sight of herself in an enormous gilt-framed mirror. Except for poor images in the glass of shop windows, it was the first time for ages Sky had seen her true reflection.

It was like coming across someone she hadn't seen for years. Her face was much thinner than she remembered it, making her firm jawline even more pronounced. That, and the boyish hairstyle which Berry kept giving her, only served to strengthen her resemblance to her father. But, in spite of everything, Sky was amazed how well she looked. Leaner, but much much fitter.

"If only I felt as tough and as sure of myself as I look," she murmured to her reflection.

"Are you coming, or what?" Spindor called and Sky ran downstairs to join him.

"So what do you think of the place?" Spindor asked. Sitting in the shade of a big old tree, they had finished all the food and he was lying back against

141

the trunk, gazing at the house whilst drinking long swigs of beer from a can.

"It's beautiful," Sky sighed. She was lying on her stomach in the grass amongst the remnants of their picnic.

"Then will you and Chip come and live here?"

"Who else is coming?"

Spindor shook his head. "Haven't decided. I wanted to start off with you two and get the place fixed up a bit before I start bringing more. Eventually I reckon there could be as many as twenty but, apart from anything else, I think it'll be easier to persuade kids to come when I've actually left the Protection Unit. Look at the trouble I'm having convincing you!"

"It's just that I keep thinking, everything seems too perfect, there's got to be a snag."

"That's the trouble with living on the street for too long. You reach a point where you don't trust anybody. That's why I'd prefer to rescue kids who haven't been out there long, instead of the really hardened types."

"But Dig would really love to come and live in a place like this."

"Yes, Dig. You keep mentioning him."

"He's always wanted to live in the country. All the walls of the inside of his hut are covered in pictures of the countryside. He'd be useful too, he's very practical, like you."

"Maybe I should talk to Dig," Spindor said thoughtfully. "Perhaps you could arrange a meeting?"

Spindor's suggestion made Sky feel much happier. "If Dig agrees to come and live here, then we certainly will," she added.

"Why did you ask Berry to look after me if you aren't thinking of leaving me behind?" Chip asked for the second time. He fixed Sky with a stern look and yet

142

managed at the same time to look hurt and vulnerable. Dig was watching her too, but he didn't speak.

She'd spent the whole of the journey back worrying over how she was going to broach the subject with the others, especially Chip and Dig. In the end she hadn't had much choice.

They'd been late starting back from the farmhouse, both being reluctant to leave such a perfect spot. So, by the time they'd got back to the city and she'd crossed the tracks and got down to their hut, there was no sign of Chip. She went straight round to Dig's and there he was, very upset.

Apparently he'd got home from Picking, found no sign of Sky and gone looking for her at the standpipe. There he'd bumped into Berry, who'd promptly told him what his sister had said the previous night and he'd run straight to Dig and told him that he thought Sky had left without him.

"It isn't like that at all," Sky said, trying to calm him down. She'd hoped to talk to Dig and Chip separately, but there was no hope of that now. "Look, it's like this . . ." she said and launched into the whole story.

She told them everything about Spindor offering them a new life. She explained her fears about going on the journey and why she'd said what she had to Berry. Then she described, in detail, the wonderful farmhouse, tucked away in the beautiful valley. Of course the last bit was really for Dig's benefit, because she ended with Spindor's invitation for Dig to meet him and talk it over.

When she'd finished there was silence for a few moments before Chip said, "It wouldn't be the same as working on the Tip, but it sounds okay to me."

Dig still didn't speak.

"Dig, what are you thinking?" Sky asked.

He shrugged. "Like you, there has to be a catch."

143

"But there isn't!" Sky insisted. "If he'd wanted to kidnap me he could have done it without any problem this afternoon, or he could have insisted on Chip coming too and got us both."

"So what does he want to talk to me about?"

"I said we'd definitely go if you would. Dig, it's a terrific chance to get a fresh start and you know how much you've always wanted to go and live in the country. We couldn't possibly go without you, not after all you've done for us, it just wouldn't be fair."

"I don't like it," he said quietly, "there's something not quite right. Catchers don't do this kind of thing."

"I know, that's what I thought too, but he's giving up the job and sooner or later you've got to trust somebody. So what's the harm in talking?"

"Okay," he finally agreed, "but I still don't like it."

Seventeen

"Is it true you're leaving?" Jeans asked one evening when he arrived, ahead of the others, for his usual lessons.

"Who told you that?" Sky asked.

"Word's going round that you two are going away. Is it true?"

"Nothing's been decided yet," she said firmly.

Despite repeated reminders and broken dates, three weeks had passed since Sky's visit to the farmhouse and Dig still hadn't talked to Spindor. At the end of the week Spindor would be leaving his job and the city for good, but Sky refused to commit herself to going with him until he'd discussed it with Dig.

Jeans stared at Sky. "But you *are* thinking about moving on, aren't you?"

"Yes, Jeans, we are."

"I can't say I blame you. If I got the chance I'd be off like a shot. Even so . . ." Jeans ground to a halt.

"What?" Sky was fairly certain she knew what he was about to say.

He shifted uneasily. "Oh, I don't know. We're going to miss you."

"We're going to miss everybody here too, but what you're really talking about is the lessons, isn't it?"

"Not just the lessons," he grinned, "but, yes. I've been getting on really well since you started teaching us and if you go that'll all end."

"It doesn't have to, Jeans. It's mostly a question of practice. Besides, you could get somebody else to help you, Berry for instance."

"Everybody else is always too busy and the trouble is I probably won't bother. I'll hate myself, but I'll just let everything slide again."

"You know there's always one other alternative," said Sky.

"Yes, I know," Jeans groaned. "Go and ask the monks if they'll have me back again at the orphanage."

"Surely it wasn't so bad and anyway, better than losing out altogether?"

"I suppose you're right," Jeans sighed. "At least when I come out I won't have to cope with the problems kids who've spent their whole lives in there have to face."

"I don't understand."

"They're forced to leave when they're sixteen but they're so used to being in there, they come out with no experience of life outside. They can't make the simplest decisions for themselves. Some of them don't last five minutes. Fact is, they just aren't street-smart like me." Jeans sighed. "It's just that with you teaching us, I've had the best of both worlds, know what I mean?"

Sky smiled. "Yes, I do, but the monks can teach you far more than I can and there's much more to learn than just reading and writing."

"Maybe I'll give it another shot," Jeans agreed. Then, as the others drifted up, he added quickly, "But like I said, I still think you should go if you get the chance."

"If" was the crucial word! The last time she'd bumped into Spindor he seemed to be taking her slowness to accept his invitation as showing lack of enthusiasm for leaving the Tip.

"I'm not trying to force you two into anything," he'd said. "If you don't want to go, there's plenty of others that will."

"I do want us to go," she'd insisted. "It's just that I want you to talk to Dig first."

"Can't you make up your own mind? Seems to me it's no contest if all you've got to choose between is living in a shanty scavenging on the Tip when you could have a decent life in a real house in the country."

How could she tell him it wasn't that simple? That she *didn't* trust her own judgement. She needed Dig to reassure her that going with Spindor was the right thing to do. She hated the idea of being, even for the first few weeks, alone with Spindor except for Chip. She couldn't forget Stin leering at Childie and she wanted Dig with them. There might be safety in numbers.

Not that Spindor had ever suggested anything more than talking to Dig. Whenever he mentioned them going with him it was always, "you two", but Sky had tended to dismiss that as nothing more than a figure of speech.

But there was something else. Nothing more than an idea which hovered in the darkest corners of her mind, something she couldn't give shape to and certainly wouldn't have been able to put into words. But that shadow, whatever it was, took the shine off the whole idea for Sky and prevented her from giving a final answer until after Dig and Spindor met. If the doubt she suffered was justified, she knew she could rely on Dig to sniff out the reason, but if her fears proved groundless, then they could go ahead.

"I'll make sure he talks to you," she'd promised.

"There's only seven more days before I'm out of here," Spindor had cautioned.

"I know, I know!"

* * *

After the lesson ended, Sky made her way down to Dig's hut. As the sun started to set a strong wind began to blow in from the west, coming directly across the Tip making the unpleasant smell even stronger than usual.

"I shan't be sorry to get away from that!" she said, wrinkling her nose. She found Dig outside his hut, loading scrap metal into his cart.

"You're determined to go through with this idea then?" Dig said, straightening his back.

"Only after you've met Spindor and said everything's all right. I've said that all along."

"But you want to go, don't you?"

"Yes, but I also want you to come too and you can't decide either way until you've talked with him. But Spindor leaves the day after tomorrow and if we don't go with him we could be missing the chance of a lifetime."

"That's the part that bothers me," Dig said thoughtfully.

"What do you mean?"

"People, especially Catchers, never offer Throwaways 'the chance of a lifetime'. Not without some enormous snag!"

"I know but if there is one I can't find it. Which is why I want you to go and talk to Spindor, so that if it's a good deal we won't miss out on it."

"All right! I've got to go with this load of scrap tomorrow."

"Good! Shakey's got his regular date with his ladyfriend at five, so Spindor'll be parked in his usual spot behind the baker's."

"Okay, I'll be there," Dig said.

But he didn't sound very enthusiastic and so Sky pressed him. "You won't forget?"

"No! Were you a pirate in a previous life?"

"What makes you ask?"

"Because I think you'd have been very good at making people walk the plank!"

Sky laughed and left him, but the next afternoon she returned, just in case he'd forgotten. She banged on the door, there was no reply.

Jeans popped his head out of a nearby hut. "If you're looking for Dig, he's already gone. Look," he said, pointing to the top of the hill, "you can just see him now."

Sky shaded her eyes against the sun and made out the unmistakable figure of Dig walking alongside the chain-link fence. Despite the heat, he was still wearing his threadbare, brown sweater and was bent forwards as he pushed the heavy cart up the steep, uneven track.

At that distance Dig looked so small, no bigger than a speck and she suddenly wished she'd gone with him, but it was too late.

"I bet he's doing this on purpose," Sky said bitterly.

"What? Who?" Chip spluttered through a mouthful of bread. "Who's doing what?"

"Dig. He's probably been back ages, but he's staying away on purpose because I nagged him so much."

"He wouldn't do that," Chip said loyally.

"Oh, yes, he would! I'm going down to his place."

"But you haven't finished eating."

"You have it, I'm not hungry."

"All right!" Chip said, snatching up her crust before she'd left.

But when she arrived at Dig's hut there was no sign of him, or his cart.

"No," Jeans said, "I haven't seen him since we watched him going up the hill this afternoon."

Sky went all round the camp, but nobody had talked to Dig since midday.

"I'm sure something's gone wrong," she said to Derry. "I wish I'd gone with him."

"Oh, no. You know Dig, he's probably found himself a good meal somewhere! He'll be back, you'll see."

But when he still hadn't returned the following morning Sky was ragged with worry and insisted Chip should come with her to search for him in the city.

"You're worrying about nothing," Chip kept saying. "This isn't the first time Dig's spent a night away. He knows plenty of safe places, like the Jungle. He's quite capable of looking after himself. Better than us."

Sky ignored him. Something told her Dig was in trouble and she wouldn't rest until she found him. "We'll start by going up to the scrap yard."

The Tin Man told them, "Dig was in here soon after three. I bought quite a lot off him. I remember 'im particular, 'cos he took a packet of money off me."

"Maybe he got robbed," Sky wondered out loud as they left. "Perhaps he's lying hurt somewhere."

"It'd take an army, Dig's too smart to get caught like that," Chip replied.

"In that case where is he?" Chip shook his head. "Where might he have gone after this?"

Chip thought for a moment and then his face brightened. "If Dig had money, the first thing he'd do would be to go and buy something to eat."

"And if he intended to meet Spindor," Sky said hopefully, "maybe he called in at the baker's on the way! Come on!"

They ran all the way to Doughy's and burst through the back door into his hot kitchen. Doughy looked up, startled.

"Did Dig come here yesterday, Doughy?"

"Yes, he did. Bought something too, which quite surprised me. Usually he's after something for

150

nothing, like the rest of you, but this time he bought some cakes."

"So," Chip said triumphantly to Sky, "we know he hadn't been robbed by the time he got here."

"Robbed? How do you mean?" Doughy looked baffled.

"No time to explain," Sky said, pulling Chip after her.

Doughy wasn't used to people coming and going like that. "Here! There's some stale rolls on the side you can have."

Chip would have loved one, but Sky wouldn't wait. Instead she dragged him out to the road at the end of the entry, where Spindor always parked while Shakey went off to see his lady-friend.

"I bet Spindor's behind this!" Sky said bitterly.

"Sky, you don't even know that they met."

"Just wait until I see him, that's all!"

But that didn't happen until the end of the afternoon, by which time they'd searched everywhere, getting tired, hungry and more worried by the second, without finding the slightest clue to Dig's whereabouts.

They bumped into Spindor, still dressed in civilian clothes, on his way to check on for his very last night shift as a Catcher.

Sky ran straight up to him and began to beat his chest with her clenched fists. "Where's Dig? What have you done to him?"

As Chip caught up, Spindor grabbed Sky by the wrists and tried to calm her down. "Hey, come on now! What's all this about?"

Sky's tears were only partially caused by anger. "Dig," she sobbed. "He came to meet you yesterday and he hasn't been seen since."

"Did you tell him to meet me behind Doughy's?"

"Yes, just like always."

151

"Well, I haven't seen him either."

"I don't believe you," she shouted.

"Believe what you like, honey, but I'm telling you, I was there at the usual time and he didn't show up."

"Then what's happened to him?"

Spindor stirred his chewing gum around his mouth for a few moments. "I'm on my way in to work. I can ask around, check yesterday's files. Maybe somebody picked him up."

"We're coming with you," Sky said defiantly.

"You do that and you'll get picked up anyway."

"I'm not leaving until I know what's happened to Dig."

"Suit yourself, only keep out of sight. Or tomorrow you could end up somewhere you've no intention of going."

Eighteen

While Spindor ran up the steps and went into the sombre-looking building which housed the headquarters of the Child Protection Unit, Sky and Chip slipped down a side street to crouch back in a doorway at the rear.

Chip suspiciously eyed the grey building, most of its windows covered by drawn blinds. "Do you think Dig's locked up in there?"

"I just don't know what to believe any more," Sky said, but she too found it very scary, being so close to the one building every child she knew tried to avoid visiting.

She couldn't help wondering exactly who was locked in the wire cages of the black vans which nosed their way ominously under a barrier as they passed in and out of the yard. It was guarded by two armed Catchers who thoroughly checked everything that moved against the lists on their clipboard.

An uneasy half hour passed. Darkness began to fall. Sky slumped down on her haunches and Chip hopped nervously from foot to foot, asking every few seconds, "What do you think's keeping Spindor?"

Just as Sky was beginning to give up hope, Spindor, who'd changed into his uniform, flashed his identity card at one of the guards and sauntered across the road.

"Not here, round the corner!" he hissed at Sky out

153

of the side of his mouth as he passed their doorway
without glancing in their direction.

A couple of minutes elapsed before they slipped out
of the shadows and followed him. He appeared to be
browsing through the magazines which festooned all
four sides of the newsvendor's kiosk, a wooden shack
standing on the edge of the pavement. Spindor didn't
look up from the contents of the motorcycle magazine
he was studying as they edged up beside him and
pretended to look at pop magazines.

"Sorry it took so long," he said quietly, without
lifting his eyes from the page, "but I checked all the
files and the Daily Report Book. There was no mention, in any of them, of Dig being picked up
yesterday."

"I don't believe you," Sky insisted, "there must be!"

"Look, Sky," Spindor sighed impatiently, "anything
could have happened. You said he had money on him;
he might have been mugged. And what about Dozer?
He'd threatened to get his own back on Dig and
judging by the way Dozer tried to get rid of you, that
could have unpleasant results. Or Dig might simply
have taken off on his own. Kids disappear off the
streets all the time and although we always get
blamed, half the time it's nothing to do with us."

"I don't believe he'd just go off on his own," Chip
said.

"Why not? Maybe he didn't want to come with you,
but neither liked to say so, nor to stand in your way."

"But why wouldn't he want to come?" Sky asked.
"He *loved* the countryside. But maybe he found some
catch in what you're offering us. I couldn't convince
him it was just the opportunity we'd all been hoping
for."

When the kiosk's owner poked his head out Spindor
moved away, further along the rack and began to
riffle through a copy of *Time* magazine. "Sky, some

people just aren't prepared to be brought face to face with their dreams. To them dreams are nothing more than something to cling on to while they struggle through the day, but when they're offered the opportunity to live them, they take fright. Not like me and you, I hope."

"We can't walk out on Dig!" Sky protested.

"But you don't know that he hasn't done exactly that to you," Spindor pointed out.

Sky didn't know what to say. "It's just not like him."

Spindor shrugged. "All street kids get like that after a while, believe me. It goes with the life style – unreliable." He dropped the magazine, left it swinging by its hook and turned to face Sky. "I've got to get back on duty. As this is my last shift, there's a lot of odds and ends to clear up. Tomorrow, first thing, straight after work, I leave for the farm. I'd like you and Chip to be going with me. But, if you are coming, be sure to be at the car park by ten, or else forget it!" Without waiting for a reply Spindor turned on his heels and walked off back to the yard.

They were taking a short cut back across a patch of waste ground, heading for the sidings when Chip, who was running ahead along the tops of some hillocks, suddenly called out, "Sky! Look here!"

Sky searched the uneven tufted grass, littered with broken bottles and wastepaper, but away from the street lights it was impossible to see what had caught Chip's attention.

He'd run down into a slight dip and was waving his arms frantically. "Quick, down here!"

Sky followed, thinking it was probably only some wonderful piece of scrap which he'd found, but when she reached the edge of the hollow and looked down, she stopped dead.

155

Beside Chip, lying on its side, was Dig's cart. One wheel was buckled, the other missing entirely and both handles had been snapped off short.

Sky slithered down the slope to join him. Together they silently stared at the remains. Sky felt a little like a nosy pedestrian hanging round the scene of a traffic accident, though in this case it was worse because she knew the victim well.

"The paint's all scratched," Chip said in a hushed whisper. "What happened?"

Sky shook her head. She didn't trust herself to speak rationally. What she wanted to do was let out a huge wail of anguish.

Chip just went on staring. "It looks as if a truck's hit it."

"You couldn't get a truck over here," she snapped.

"What about the Hooligans in one of those beach buggies? They go anywhere."

"This ground's too rough, even for them."

"So?"

"Shut up and let me think!" she snapped again, suspicions sliding round in her head like snakes. Finally she said, "Whatever happened, I don't believe it was here. Somebody brought the hand-cart here, thinking nobody would find it and in a way I wish we hadn't."

"Why?"

"Because it doesn't tell us what's happened to Dig, does it? He might not have even been with the cart when all this damage was done. Maybe he left it somewhere else and some kids ran off with it and smashed it up before they dumped it here. I don't know." Her voice tailed off.

Although she hated looking at the broken cart, she found it impossible to drag her eyes away from the remains. Sky could not face the horrible facts they suggested, that Dig might have met a similar fate and at that very moment his maimed body could be lying half-hidden somewhere in the city.

The run of paint beneath the G in his name seemed to turn into a tear and she shivered. "There's nothing more we can do here," she said, "we may as well go home."

"Maybe Dig will be sitting in our hut," Chip suggested hopefully.

"I doubt it," Sky replied softly. The wrecked cart had finally banished any hope she'd clung to of ever seeing Dig again.

When they got back Chip burst into their hut full of expectation, but Dig wasn't there. He ran down to Dig's hut, but it was still empty and nobody had seen him.

Neither of them felt hungry. They sat in their hut silently watching the flickering flame of the lamp until Chip said, "What are we going to do? Are we going with Spindor?"

"I don't think we've got much choice. We can't live here for years, waiting for one of us to be buried by a landslide on the Tip. We'd always be dreading what people like Dozer might do. What happens when the Hooligans turn up again to smash the huts? And what about the Catchers? You've got to remember whatever's happened to Dig, it could be our turn next."

"I suppose you're right." Chip looked around him. "We'd better pack."

Sky looked round the hut. "There's nothing I want to take, apart from any food we've got left." For Sky one of the attractions of starting a new life with Spindor was that she could leave all her possessions behind. After all, they'd arrived at the Tip with nothing, why take anything away?

Sky envied snakes. She would have loved to have

been able to cast her old skin before leaving the Tip. "The moment we've gone somebody else will move in here and they can probably use most of this stuff. There's nothing you want to take, is there?"

Chip was surprised to find there wasn't, although later Sky noticed him slip the makeshift knife Dig had made for him and the battered toy car, which she didn't know he'd kept, into his pocket as reminders of his previous lives.

"Do you think we ought to go and say goodbye to everyone?" he asked.

Sky knew, if she had to face everybody and their questions about Dig, what little resolve she'd managed to summon up would quickly crumble. "No," she said firmly, adding, "it isn't like being at a party where you have to say 'thank you for having me'! I bet you, by the end of next week they'll all have completely forgotten us. I remember once seeing a car drive off the road. It hit a hedge, forced its way through and then the hedge simply closed up behind it, as if the car had never existed. It'll be like that with us, the moment somebody moves in here. Come on, we'd better turn in soon, we can't afford to be late tomorrow."

When they were lying in bed with the light out Chip whispered, "Sky, are you asleep yet?"

"Not yet."

"Tell me again about the farm."

Sky launched quite happily into a long and detailed description of the farmhouse, beginning outside and then moving through it room by room. Then something curious and disturbing happened. As she pictured each room, they were still all empty, apart from Dig. Wherever she went and however quickly she moved around the house, she was unable to shake him off.

She tried desperately to comfort herself with the

thought of soaking in that wonderful bath, but to hold on to the image, she felt she must share that too with Chip. "And there's this fantastic bath we can use," she said. "Chip, are you listening?"

But Chip was fast asleep and Sky lay awake until just before dawn with the haunting picture of Dig wandering from room to room, pausing only to look out of the windows, as if he was searching for them in the empty house. A house which she knew he would never see in real life, even though his ghost might inhabit it for ever.

Nineteen

Spindor looked both surprised and pleased when his white pick-up turned into the car park and he found Sky already waiting for him with Chip beside her. "Silly question really, but no luggage?"

Sky held up a carrier bag. "Just some food, in case we had to wait for you, and a few clothes." She hadn't wanted to bring anything from the hut but finally, realising it might be a while before Spindor could buy any, she'd decided spare clothes were essential.

"Okay, hop on board!"

Chip eagerly scrambled up in to the cab and settled on the bench seat next to Spindor. "This truck's just like my toy one," he said, "except for the colour."

The bleak life he'd led during the last few months had in no way dulled Chip's sense of adventure. Not only was he looking forward to the drive, the first he'd had since they'd come to the city, but he couldn't wait to get out in the fields and meadows Sky had described. Although there had been one or two outings while they'd been living on the Tip, those had only been to city parks at weekends, when they could safely mingle amongst the crowds. Somehow those had always been tinged with sadness when he'd noticed that most of the other kids had their mums and dads with them.

Sky climbed up more slowly and as she pulled the door to after her, still expecting something to go wrong, she felt that she was closing off a segment of

160

her life. This was how her parents must have felt when they shut their car door the night they left.

It was a bright sunny morning. Once the truck was moving and nothing could stop them, she should have been happy. After all, she'd got her way. She was leaving the Tip, somewhere she'd always hated, for good.

And yet, while Chip and Spindor sang silly songs at the tops of their voices, Sky stayed silent, watching the road ahead. Chip didn't even notice when they passed the spot where their own car had last rested.

"Still thinking about your friend?" Spindor asked in a break between songs. Sky nodded. "I shouldn't worry your head about him any more. He'll be fine. I tell you what, he's probably pushing his hand-cart through town right this minute."

There was a long silence during which Sky felt as if a long, ice-cold knife had been thrust through her stomach. "How did you know Dig had a cart?" she asked quietly.

Spindor, hiding behind his sunglasses, kept his eyes on the road. "What?"

"You never met him, remember?"

"No, but the lads said he had one." Spindor still looked casual, one arm resting on the open window, but his voice sounded less steady. "What's the big deal?"

"It's just that, after we left you last night, we found Dig's cart. It was all smashed up and somebody had dumped it on a patch of waste ground."

"Really?"

Sky watched Spindor very closely. "You wouldn't know anything about that?"

"Course not!"

"Pull over," Sky said suddenly.

"Why?" Spindor sounded as if he was determined to brazen out whatever was coming.

"Because I'm getting out of this truck unless you tell me the truth. You can either pull over," she said, reaching for the door handle, "or I'll jump out while it's still moving."

"You're crazy!" Spindor tried to laugh, but he sounded concerned. "You'll kill yourself."

Instead of answering, Sky tugged on the handle and struggled to push open the door against the slipstream until she could see, through the gap, the tarmac and gravel speeding past beneath them.

Spindor's nerve cracked when Sky eased herself forwards in her seat and looked about to jump. "Okay!" he said, applying the brakes and swinging the wheel over so abruptly that Sky lost her balance and was thrown forwards against the dashboard.

As Sky picked herself up, Spindor switched off the engine.

Chip, who'd been looking from one to the other, couldn't take the silence which followed and broke it. "What happened?"

Spindor pushed his sunglasses up on to the top of his head and then anxiously wiped his hand over his face. "You've got to understand, it wasn't my fault and there was nothing I could do to stop it."

Sky stared blindly at the distant horizon. Her voice was very flat. "What wasn't your fault?"

"Dig got picked up two days ago."

"Who by?"

"Shakey."

"So you were there too!"

"Yes, in a way. What happened was, Shakey's lady-friend wasn't well. He came back early to the van and walked slap into Dig before I could do anything to warn the kid. And that's the honest truth."

"What happened to Dig?"

162

"Does that matter?" Spindor sounded uncomfortable. "What's done is done."

But Sky insisted on probing Spindor's open wound. "Tell me what happened to him."

Spindor cleared his throat whilst searching for the words which would let Sky down gently. "Shakey had a contract . . ."

"Who with?"

"Look, it's for the best, Sky. Dig hasn't come out of it badly."

Sky pressed on. "Who was the contract with?"

"Some farmer, hundreds of miles from here. That's what I mean, Dig got his wish. He's ended up living in the country."

"You've sold Dig as a slave!" Sky hissed out the word at Spindor, hardly able to believe what he was saying.

"Oh, come on, at least it won't be as bad as the sweatshop Dozer sent you to."

"But Dig isn't free any more, is he?" Sky said.

Spindor shook his head.

Suddenly the shadow, which had lurked in the back of Sky's mind ever since Spindor had first talked about going to the farm, developed a recognisable and ugly shape. Sky snatched up the bags and jumped down on to the roadside. "Chip, get out of the truck."

Spindor reached out and gently stopped Chip from moving. "Wait a minute, there's no need to behave like that."

"There's every need," Sky said, trembling with controlled anger. "No doubt your friend Shakey cut you in on the money he got from selling Dig?"

Spindor avoided Sky's searching gaze. "I explained that to you before. The money just gets paid into my account, I don't even know who by."

"Just like it has for all the other kids who've been sold off like cattle? Well, I can't build a new life on the blood money that's come from other people's misery and suffering; your share of the drugs money, of the foreign adoption fees, or the selling of innocent kids into slavery, like you've done with Dig."

Spindor was desperate to prove his innocence. "I told you, it wasn't me, it was Shakey who did that."

"But you were there, just as you were all the other times and you could have done *something* to stop it happening. Instead you've always taken your cut and now you've settled your conscience by using it to buy the farm."

"I haven't spent a penny of that money on myself, it's all gone into the farm project and it'll be used to help rescue more kids."

"You want to rescue somebody?" she screamed at him, the anger she felt was turning into bitter hatred. "Then rescue Dig!"

He pleaded for her understanding. "You know I can't do that. Look, Sky, I know in a perfect world we'd all behave better towards each other but at least, in my case, you've got to agree, the end justifies the means."

"No, I don't. The trouble is you've spent too long with the Catchers and although you don't approve of what they do, you've got tainted by their thinking. It didn't hit me until now, now that it's happened to Dig: nothing can justify accepting money for what you've done to all those poor kids and I don't want any part in it. I'd never be able to live in that beautiful farmhouse knowing what misery, particularly Dig's, helped you to buy it. Chip, are you coming with me, or going with him?" It was a terrible moment, she didn't know what his reply would be.

But before Chip could answer, Spindor cut in quickly, "But where will you go, back to the Tip?"

"No," she said without hesitation, "I don't know

about Chip, but I know I'm not strong enough to live through that kind of life and come out unscarred."

"Then where?"

"We'll make our own way somehow. We'll survive, don't worry about us."

"Look," he said, in one last desperate effort to persuade her, "I'm sorry for what happened, but you're making too big an issue out of it, honey. You and I both wish things in society weren't the way they are, but we still have to deal with the real world and that was my way of handling it. The best way I knew how. Don't let something I've done ruin your chances, come with me."

A fleeting image of what she was giving up, the farmhouse surrounded by fields, the garden and, above all, that glorious bath, passed through her brain, but Sky's mind was made up and she shook her head. "I could never enjoy my freedom knowing I'd got it at the expense of Dig's. Besides, how could I ever trust you again? After all, you're no more morally honest than our own parents, are you? If times got hard you might even think about selling *us* off!"

Spindor was genuinely horrified. "Never. I swear I've never sold anyone in my life and anyway I've left all that behind me now."

"How do you know? Just suppose the project isn't as self-supporting as you'd hoped and you'd reached the point where you had to make a choice; you could either lose the farm, or sell just one more kid. Are you absolutely positive you wouldn't be tempted?" Spindor shook his head, but he didn't speak and Sky held her hand out to Chip. "Are you coming?"

Chip wriggled free of Spindor's arm and slid along the seat towards his sister murmuring unhappily, "Dig was my best friend."

As she helped Chip down on to the road, Sky

noticed that silent tears were streaming down her brother's face and she wondered how she could have ever doubted where his loyalty lay.

When Sky slammed the door Spindor, looking tired and drained, leaned over and thrust his head out of the open window. "Look, Sky, I'm not Superman. I'm an ordinary guy trying to make the best of life. I did the best I could."

"I know. Maybe I expect too much," Sky half apologised, "but it's the way I am."

"Which is why I chose you in the first place!" Spindor laughed bitterly. "Ironic, isn't it? I wanted you to come because you were honest and now you won't come because I'm not honest enough for you! Look, if you ever change your mind, or you need any help, you know where I'll be."

"If I wanted help I'd sooner find Dig than you," Sky said defiantly.

Spindor shook his head. "Sorry, I can't help you there, I've no idea where Shakey sent him."

"Never mind, we'll probably come across him one day and even if we don't, we'll still make out."

"I'm sorry it's got to end like this, but maybe it's only what I deserve. I promise you, nothing like it will ever happen again," Spindor said. "Good luck, I really mean that, both of you!"

"And you," Sky said. "After all, you won't be short of kids for the project and it is a wonderful thing you're doing for them."

"I just wish I could have made it right for you, Sky," Spindor said. Then he pulled his head in, started the engine, threw the truck into gear and drove off.

As the noise of the engine faded into the distance Chip looked at Sky. "So, what *do* we do now?"

Sky smiled uncertainly at him. "I don't know, but it won't be like last time, not after everything Dig

166

taught us." She was beginning to realise just how much they relied on each other, which produced a surge of guilt when she remembered how near she'd come to abandoning Chip the day her parents left them. "We'll manage somehow and at least we'll both have clear consciences!"

"That's right!" Chip agreed enthusiastically.

"Come on, let's go," Sky said. She knew they were following Spindor's route, but that was simply because it led away from all the dangers of city life and she was determined to find her own turning off it.

After a few steps Chip said, "My feet hurt."

Sky turned and was about to shout at him until she realised he was smiling.

"Only kidding," he said, quietly sneaking his hand into hers as they walked side by side up the road.

General Editors: Anne and Ian Serraillier

Chinua Achebe Things Fall Apart
Douglas Adams The Hitchhiker's Guide to the Galaxy
Vivien Alcock The Cuckoo Sister; The Monster Garden; The Trial of Anna Cotman; A Kind of Thief
Margaret Atwood The Handmaid's Tale
J G Ballard Empire of the Sun
Nina Bawden The Witch's Daughter; A Handful of Thieves; Carrie's War; The Robbers; Devil by the Sea; Kept in the Dark; The Finding; Keeping Henry; Humbug
E R Braithwaite To Sir, With Love
John Branfield The Day I Shot My Dad
F Hodgson Burnett The Secret Garden
Ray Bradbury The Golden Apples of the Sun; The Illustrated Man
Betsy Byars The Midnight Fox; Goodbye, Chicken Little; The Pinballs
Victor Canning The Runaways; Flight of the Grey Goose
Ann Coburn Welcome to the Real World
Hannah Cole Bring in the Spring
Jane Leslie Conly Racso and the Rats of NIMH
Robert Cormier We All Fall Down
Roald Dahl Danny, The Champion of the World; The Wonderful Story of Henry Sugar; George's Marvellous Medicine; The BFG; The Witches; Boy; Going Solo; Charlie and the Chocolate Factory; Matilda
Anita Desai The Village by the Sea
Charles Dickens A Christmas Carol; Great Expectations
Peter Dickinson The Gift; Annerton Pit; Healer
Berlie Doherty Granny was a Buffer Girl
Gerald Durrell My Family and Other Animals
J M Falkner Moonfleet
Anne Fine The Granny Project
Anne Frank The Diary of Anne Frank
Leon Garfield Six Apprentices
Jamila Gavin The Wheel of Surya
Adele Geras Snapshots of Paradise

Graham Greene The Third Man and The Fallen Idol; Brighton Rock
Thomas Hardy The Withered Arm and Other Wessex Tales
Rosemary Harris Zed
L P Hartley The Go-Between
Ernest Hemingway The Old Man and the Sea; A Farewell to Arms
Nat Hentoff Does this School have Capital Punishment?
Nigel Hinton Getting Free; Buddy; Buddy's Song
Minfong Ho Rice Without Rain
Anne Holm I Am David
Janni Howker Badger on the Barge; Isaac Campion
Linda Hoy Your Friend Rebecca
Barbara Ireson (Editor) In a Class of Their Own
Jennifer Johnston Shadows on Our Skin
Toeckey Jones Go Well, Stay Well
James Joyce A Portrait of the Artist as a Young Man
Geraldine Kaye Comfort Herself; A Breath of Fresh Air
Clive King Me and My Million
Dick King-Smith The Sheep-Pig
Daniel Keyes Flowers for Algernon
Elizabeth Laird Red Sky in the Morning; Kiss the Dust
D H Lawrence The Fox and The Virgin and the Gypsy; Selected Tales
Harper Lee To Kill a Mockingbird
Julius Lester Basketball Game
Ursula Le Guin A Wizard of Earthsea
C Day Lewis The Otterbury Incident
David Line Run for Your Life; Screaming High
Joan Lingard Across the Barricades; Into Exile; The Clearance; The File on Fraulein Berg
Penelope Lively The Ghost of Thomas Kempe
Jack London The Call of the Wild; White Fang
Bernard Mac Laverty Cal; The Best of Bernard Mac Laverty
Margaret Mahy The Haunting; The Catalogue of The Universe
Jan Mark Do You Read Me? Eight Short Stories
James Vance Marshall Walkabout
Somerset Maugham The Kite and Other Stories
Michael Morpurgo Waiting for Anya; My Friend Walter; The War of Jenkins' Ear

How many have you read?